'Can't we be [...] we were bef[...] happened we [...] sorts. If you'd stayed we might have been able to comfort each other.'

'But I didn't, did I?' he said. 'I left you to cope on your own…and yours was a double loss.'

'And a gain. I've got Jessica, don't forget. Why don't you come round some time and meet her?'

'All right. I will. I have your address somewhere.' He wasn't going to tell her that he knew it off by heart. 'Bye for now, Fabia.'

As she placed her hand in his she hoped that he couldn't feel her trembling. Hope was being born again. Bryce was back in her life. For how long she didn't know. But just the fact that he'd come in from the wilderness was enough to make her heart leap in her breast.

Abigail Gordon loves to write about the fascinating combination of medicine and romance from her home in a Cheshire village. She is active in local affairs and is even called upon to write the script for the annual village pantomime! Her eldest son is a hospital manager and helps with all her medical research. As part of a close-knit family, she treasures having two of her sons living close by and the third one not too far away. This also gives her the added pleasure of being able to watch her delightful grandchildren growing up.

Recent titles by the same author:

THE PREGNANT POLICE SURGEON
THE NURSE'S CHILD
FIRE RESCUE

IN-FLIGHT EMERGENCY

BY
ABIGAIL GORDON

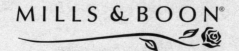

MILLS & BOON®

First published in Great Britain 2003
Harlequin Mills & Boon Limited,
Eton House, 18-24 Paradise Road, Richmond, Surrey TW9 1SR

© Abigail Gordon 2003

ISBN 0 263 83473 5

Set in Times Roman 10½ on 12 pt.
03-1003-47314

Printed and bound in Spain
by Litografia Rosés, S.A., Barcelona

CHAPTER ONE

AT SEVEN o'clock on a summer morning the airport was preparing for the day ahead. It had been a busy enough night, but with daybreak the crowds of holiday travellers and business commuters would be multiplying as dozens of cars, buses and taxis brought them in and took them away.

As Fabia came down the escalator she could feel the great throbbing heartbeat of the place reaching out to her as it had done every day since she'd joined the staff of the NHS walk-in centre situated near the departure lounge.

She smiled. After five years' nursing in the subdued luxury of the private sector, the airport's noise and bustle was a welcome change. She was beginning to come alive again.

In the centre that had been provided for travellers requiring emergency health care while at the airport, it was a case of not knowing what was going to confront them next. An intriguing uncertainty that was very different from the regimented routine of hospital care, and she was loving every minute of it.

Its facilities were available to airport staff and the public from seven in the morning until ten o'clock at night, and out of hours there was always a nurse on standby.

The staff consisted of a project manager, ten experienced nurses working on a rota system, all of them with the rank of junior sister or higher, an administrator and a receptionist.

In the weeks since she'd started there Fabia had seen a smattering of everything, including an air purser who'd thought she was starting with shingles and hadn't had time to see her GP between flights and parents with pale-faced children suffering from a range of mostly minor upsets. There had also been a case of appendicitis that had been manifesting itself on an inward flight and had suddenly worsened as a teenage girl had been leaving the airport. Once Fabia had examined the girl, an ambulance had been sent for immediately.

Anxiety attacks were not uncommon, arising from the fear of flying, the strain of delayed flights, lost luggage and the general stress of checking in and becoming airbound.

The nurses didn't hand out prescriptions. But if medication was urgently required on the spot, a written request from the nurse dealing with the patient to the project manager would be acted upon and temporary treatment provided.

Occasionally a pilot would seek their assistance, charismatic in his smart gold-braided uniform and always creating a stir of interest amongst the nursing personnel.

Not where she was concerned, though, Fabia thought as she swung open the plate glass doors that led to a smart reception area which fronted management and administration offices and the two consulting rooms where patients were seen.

Since Nick's death she'd never allowed herself the time or the inclination to get involved with the opposite sex again. The hurt and misery of what had happened six years ago was only just beginning to ease, and if she'd wanted to put it behind her she couldn't, as there was always Jessica to remind her.

Jessica, bright and beautiful, had been his legacy to her. The daughter who was her reason for living. Her friend Maggie from next door had her in the mornings after Fabia had left for the airport and during school holidays. In term time she took little Jess to school, along with her own two boys. In the afternoons Fabia was able to pick up her daughter herself.

The trainee nurse who was doing reception duties for six months flashed a smile across as Fabia went past, noting the tall slenderness and golden fairness of the most reticent member of staff and wishing that she were as blessed with nature's gifts as Fabia Ferguson.

Giles Grainger, a senior nursing manager, was in charge of the walk-in centre, and as the newest member of his staff went to change into her uniform in the small room reserved for personnel use, the receptionist wasn't the only one who was aware of her arrival.

Giles was a genial, middle-aged father of teenage children, married to a local GP and totally contented with his lot. Which made him wish that Fabia looked a bit happier with what life had handed out to her, whatever it was.

Giles knew she had a child, and that to all outward appearances there was no man in her life, but that was her business and if she wanted to keep it that way she was entitled to. But he did wish that she would mix with the others a bit more.

She was excellent at her job, one of the best nurses he'd ever worked with, and what a stunner! It was incredible that she was on her own.

The day progressed like any other day since Fabia had started at the centre. There was a fourteen-year-old boy, brought in by his anxious parents with a very swollen face. It transpired that he'd collided head on with a friend while playing football earlier in the week and the two boys had nearly knocked themselves out on impact.

Jonathan had ended up with one of the other boy's teeth embedded in his forehead, causing a deep puncture and on the day of the accident had been taken to A and E. There he'd been given antibiotics to prevent any infection from bacteria on the tooth and had been taking the medication until the previous day when his GP had suggested he come off it because it had been making him feel ill.

The severe facial swelling had appeared on the way to the airport and his frantic parents were anxious to know why, and would he be at risk flying to Florida in that condition for the family's holiday?

'In answer to your questions,' Fabia told them after she'd examined the boy, 'I don't know why your son's face has swollen like it has. It could be a number of things.

'With regard to whether it is safe for him to fly, I would say no, not until he's been seen by a doctor.'

As the dismayed parents eyed each other, she asked, 'How long before your flight?'

'Four hours,' she was told.

'Then I suggest that you drive into the city centre and take him to Accident and Emergency at a hospital there. If you explain about the flight they might give you priority. But I really don't advise you to fly until a doctor has given the go-ahead.'

She flashed them a sympathetic smile and the boy smiled back. 'At least Jonathan isn't feeling ill with whatever is wrong with him,' she went on, 'so use the next four hours to try to salvage your holiday.'

And with a gloomy nod from his father they took her advice.

A woman in her forties had knocked over a cup of coffee in one of the airport's many snack bars and had apparently scalded her hand. For once Fabia was glad of the fact that hot drinks purchased on the premises were rarely at boiling point, and after treating what was turning out to be merely painful redness of the skin, the patient left to purchase another coffee.

After another stream of minor ailments Fabia reached the end of her shift. Before gathering her belongings, she popped across to the staff delicatessen to get something for their evening meal.

When she went back into the centre a man in a pilot's uniform was standing at the desk with his back to her and the receptionist was asking in her anxious-to-please voice, 'Can I help, sir?'

'I hope so,' he said in a voice that had a familiar lilt to it, and as he raised his right hand Fabia saw that it was wrapped in a bloodstained handkerchief.

But that was only partly registering. As if he sensed that someone was behind him, he turned slowly and in that moment she realised that this day was going to end up far from ordinary.

The last time she'd seen Bryce Hollister there hadn't been any gold braid on his sleeves. He'd been wearing a white coat and there'd been a stethoscope hanging from his neck.

If she was in shock, he was even more so.

'Hell!' he breathed as the colour drained from his face. 'For a moment I thought it was her…Tiffany! That she'd come back from the dead. But it's Fabia, isn't it?'

'Yes, it is,' she croaked, as her heart pounded in

her breast. 'How long have you been…' Her voice trailed away.

'A pilot? Ever since I decided that I had to get the smell of deceit out of my nose.'

'But your career! Medicine! You gave it up?' she questioned incredulously.

He shrugged.

'I always wanted to fly and after what happened it seemed one way of getting as far away as possible. What about you? What have you been up to?'

'This and that,' she said quietly, with the feeling of unreality so strong she felt as if her legs would buckle beneath her. But the blood was still seeping through his handkerchief.

'If you'd like to come into the consulting room, I'll have a look at your hand,' she told him, with a quick glance at her watch. 'I've finished my shift, but I've got an hour to spare before I leave for home.'

'And where might that be?' Bryce asked as he followed her into one of the vacant surgeries.

'A cottage in a village just outside city limits.'

He was unwrapping his hand, and when she saw the jagged cut there Fabia asked, 'How did you do this? It might need stitching.'

'I took a knife off a lout who was waving it about in a dangerous manner. The police have got him now.'

'You always did find trouble, didn't you?' she murmured as she began to cleanse the cut with antiseptic solution.

'Only in a small way. The really big trouble I didn't have to look for. It found me.'

When Fabia raised her head she found herself looking into eyes as blue as the Cornish sea, beneath hair dark as the rocks upon the shore. What had they ever done, he and she, she thought chokingly, that the two people they cared for should have treated them so?

'So tell me, what have you been doing during the past six years?' he asked, averting his gaze from hers.

Fabia took a deep breath.

'Working for my living…and bringing up my daughter.'

'So you got married again?' he said slowly.

She shook her head.

'You didn't?'

'No. Jessica is Nick's child. I didn't know it at the time, but I was pregnant when he died in the crash.'

'Oh, hell! What a mess!' he groaned. 'You never told me.'

'Would you have wanted to know if I had? You were distraught at the time. What about you?' she asked with a quick change of subject. 'Have you found someone else?'

His smile was grim.

'No way. Not after what your sister did to me. Betrayal leaves a nasty taste in the mouth. I'm married to the job. Becoming a pilot saved my sanity. I might go back to medicine one day but, believe me, it is a long way off.

'If you and I hadn't been working such long hours back then at the Infirmary, we might have seen what was coming, but we couldn't see what was going on under our noses. Or at least I couldn't.'

'I try not to think of it,' she told him. 'One can't live in the past for ever, Bryce.'

He was eyeing her with bleak thoughtfulness.

'I'd forgotten how alike you are. You weren't twins but you might well have been. Though I suppose fa-cial resemblance and colouring doesn't make you a person who would have had an affair with her sister's husband, does it?'

Fabia felt her chest muscles tighten.

The answer to his question was, no, it didn't. But she hadn't been able to stop herself from secretly loving Bryce Hollister, the dedicated doctor who'd seemed like a rock when she'd thought of the shifting sands of her life with Nick. But she'd kept that totally to herself—there was no way she would have hurt Tiffany as her sister had hurt her.

Whether her shallow-minded husband had guessed how she'd felt about her brother-in-law she would never know. Yet it was strange that he'd turned his attentions to Tiffany.

When the police had come to her with the news that he and her sister had been killed in a car crash, initially she hadn't thought twice about the fact that they'd been together as the four of them had sometimes socialised.

But when the authorities had gone on to explain that they'd had luggage with them and flight tickets, the truth had slowly begun to sink in and, added to her grief, there had been a feeling of sick revulsion at the inference that had been there for all to see.

It had been when Bryce had found out that the balloon had gone up. He'd been desolate with grief and rage and much as she'd longed to comfort him he hadn't let her near. It had almost been as if being related to Tiffany had made her an accessory to what had happened.

He'd accepted the fact that she had also been bereaved, doubly so, but because both culprits had belonged to her, she'd sensed that he hadn't been able to stand her near him. When he'd left immediately after the funerals, without leaving an address, she'd had to accept it.

His house had been sold, his post in the coronary unit at the Infirmary filled. Three out of the quartet had gone and she'd been left to face bringing up Jessica on her own. It was small wonder that those she worked with found her hard to get to know.

'Where are *you* living these days?' she asked casually.

'I've been living and working in Spain for quite some time,' he said flatly. 'I did my pilot's training at a place called Jerez. I gained most of my experience out there and only moved back to England recently. I have a house on a new development in town.'

'Have you been to see them at the hospital since you've been back?' she questioned.

Bryce nodded. 'Yes. I called in once but most of the old staff had gone and the few who remembered me were more interested in how I felt about flying since September eleventh than the fact that I once used to work there.'

'And how do you feel about it?' she asked.

He shrugged. 'Someone has to do it, Fabia.'

She had finished dressing his hand and, looking down at the neat bandage, she told him, 'You might get away without stitches but keep an eye on the cut. We don't want it to get infected.'

'Of course,' he replied in a tone that indicated the advice was unnecessary.

He was getting to his feet, ready to depart. 'Thanks for the first aid. Nice to see you again,' he said stiffly.

As she looked into his remote blue gaze Fabia felt that she couldn't let him walk out of her life again just like that. Picking up a pad and pencil off a nearby desk, she scribbled down her address and phone number and suggested with unconscious pleading, 'Can't we keep in touch, Bryce? I know the last thing you want is to talk about old times, but we were close once, weren't we?'

It had been the kind of closeness born of a mutual respect brought about by working long hours in each other's company. And until now Fabia had long accepted that was all it would ever be as far as Bryce was concerned.

'I don't have a lot of time for socialising,' he said abruptly and then added in a softer tone, 'But take care, Fabia...you and your daughter. At least you ended up with something good out of the whole sorry mess.' And picking up the flight bag that he'd been carrying, he went, a straight-backed figure striding through Reception and out into the bustling throng.

Bryce Hollister was a Cornishman who'd come up north to practise medicine. When Fabia had known him previously, he'd been an attractive, hard-working doctor on the coronary unit, married to her younger sister, Tiffany, and madly in love with his pleasure-loving blonde wife.

She, Fabia, a nurse, had had for a husband Nick Ferguson, manager of a department store, snappy dresser and a great socialiser.

She had often thought they'd married the wrong people. Bryce had worked long hours and so had she, while both their partners had had time on their hands and the urge to be out and about instead of resting after a hard day's slog on the wards.

It had perhaps been inevitable that they should be drawn to each other, just as she'd been attracted to someone like Bryce who had been so much more on her wavelength.

She'd forgiven them long ago, but Bryce was a different matter. She sensed that nothing had changed where he was concerned. He was still the bitter, deceived person he'd been then.

But she thought, with a new lightness in her step, the fates were being kind for once. Bryce was back in her town. Not as a doctor but a pilot, and if he was going to be around in the foreseeable future it wouldn't matter if he was delivering the milk, the mail or sweeping the streets for a living, just as long as he was around.

Her step faltered as the realisation came that, although she'd given him her address, he hadn't been forthcoming with his. She'd let him walk out of the centre and might never see him again as there'd been no interest on his part in renewing their acquaintance.

As Jessica came dancing across the schoolyard towards her, Fabia's spirits lightened. Bryce had been right when he'd said that she was the only one who'd got something good out of what had happened in the past.

She was a bright, uncomplicated child, with curly brown hair and eyes to match, like Nick's. Jessica made friends easily and there were always extra mouths around the table for the evening meal. And tonight was no exception as she was bringing a friend for a sleepover.

Later, as the children were being tucked in, Fabia's mind was elsewhere. Bryce was back and if she never saw him again at least she had today's meeting to hold in her heart.

All right, he hadn't exactly fallen upon her neck

and sobbed out his contrition for the way he'd treated her all that time ago, but at least he hadn't walked out on her. He'd let her treat his hand and had been civil enough. And after all, she thought with a new fire inside her, so he should have been. *She'd* done nothing wrong back then.

Her feelings for him had been hidden away in a shuttered compartment in her mind that no one was ever going to see into.

In the days that followed any sightings of male figures wearing black uniforms with gold braid had her pulses quickening, but they were never Bryce.

Until, on a morning when the sick and suffering passing through the doors of the walk-in centre seemed to be never-ending, she looked up to find him standing by the desk in Reception, watching her with the same closed expression that had been there during their strained reunion.

As their eyes met he gave a wintry smile and her heart leapt. He took a step towards her and said in a low voice, 'I can see that you're very busy. What time do you finish?'

'In half an hour,' she breathed.

'I'd like to talk to you. What if I wait in the coffee-lounge at the end of the corridor?'

'Er…yes…all right,' she agreed, dazed by his appearance after all the days of no contact..

Fabia wasn't to know it but their previous encounter had thrown him completely off balance. He'd forgotten how alike the two sisters had been and for those first few seconds of meeting he really had thought it had been Tiffany standing there, watching him with wary violet eyes.

But his wife was dead. There wasn't a day went

by when that fact wasn't brought home to him. The lonely bed, the empty rooms. The hurt that never went away.

If Tiffany thought he'd neglected her, it certainly hadn't been for another woman. It had been because he'd been working long hours treating the sick, doing what he'd trained for. And as for that treacherous scoundrel Nick!

In the mists of anger and sorrow that had surrounded him during those dark days he'd spent little time thinking about what Fabia had been going through. But seeing her again after all this time, in graceful, golden-haired reticence, had made him see himself for what he'd been like then, a selfish beast roaring about his own hurts instead of taking time to sympathise with hers.

He'd sat deep in thought that day when he'd got home and had admitted to himself that with hindsight Fabia was a much nicer person than Tiffany had been. As much as he'd loved her, he'd known that his wife had been devious and calculating when it had suited her.

Fabia he'd accepted for what she'd been in those days, an uncomplicated, dedicated nurse…and his sister-in-law. But when they'd met again he'd seen her in a different light. She was beautiful, dignified and devoid of self-pity. He hadn't been able to get her out of his mind.

He'd read the address and phone number that Fabia had given him countless times. Had even picked up the phone to ring her. But he never had and he knew why. She would remind him of old wounds.

Yet there had remained in him the feeling that he should see her again, if only to apologise for his past selfishness. And today, on his way out of the airport, he'd succumbed.

And now, as he waited for her to appear, he hadn't a clue what he was going to say when she did.

She was smiling when she came, unable to disguise her pleasure in seeing him again, and Bryce thought achingly how beautiful she was. But he knew that it wasn't Fabia he was seeing. He was imagining that the woman standing in front of him was Tiffany, his dead wife.

It took an effort to get to his feet and conjure up pleasantness but he did it. He knew that if he let this moment pass he would need to find another opportunity and he didn't want that. He wanted to tell Fabia he was sorry for the way he'd behaved and then close the book. No raking up old embers or painful reminiscences.

'You never rang,' she chided gently when she was seated across from him.

Bryce stirred his coffee slowly.

'No. I didn't, did I? But I'm here now, aren't I?'

'What do you want of me?' Fabia said slowly. 'I'm sure it isn't just to pass the time of day.'

He shook his head.

'No. It isn't. I wanted to say sorry for the way I behaved when…'

He didn't finish the sentence and she said quietly. 'When our respective partners were killed in the act of running off together?'

'Yes, that's what I was about to say,' he agreed heavily. 'It's been on my mind for a long time.'

'Yet you did nothing about it?'

'No. I did nothing about it. But ever since we met up again I've been aware that I owe you an apology.'

'You don't owe me anything, Bryce,' she told him

levelly. 'You had more cause to be hurt and outraged than I had. You loved Tiffany a lot. More than I loved Nick, I think. We jogged along together all right, but our relationship wasn't exactly spellbinding. We were too incompatible for it to be like that.'

He smiled properly for the first time.

'Yes, I did love Tiff a lot, but we weren't always in tune with each other either. It was being made a fool of that I couldn't stand when it all came out into the open…and with her sister's husband! It wouldn't have hurt so much if she'd been having an affair with a stranger, but Nick of all people.'

'They were two of a kind,' she stated simply, 'and we were never there.'

There was bleak surprise in his glance.

'You've forgiven them, haven't you?'

'Yes. I could never have got through the past few years if I hadn't. But don't let's keep harking back to the past, Bryce,' she pleaded, and pointed to the gold bands on his arm. 'You've obviously not been standing still. As well as being a doctor, you've trained as a pilot, and I've been doing the best I can for myself and Jessica. At least we are still here, while Tiffany and Nick are long gone.'

He didn't respond to that last comment, but remarked drily, 'I might have been getting on with my life career-wise, but my private life isn't going anywhere spectacular. If *you're* generous with your forgiveness, *I'm* not.'

She reached out and took his hand in hers.

'Can't we be friends, Bryce, like we were before? There were never any hang-ups between us in the old days, and after what happened we do have a bond of sorts. If you'd stayed we might have been able to comfort each other.'

'But I didn't, did I?' he said morosely. 'I left you to cope on your own…and yours was a double loss.'

'And a gain,' she prompted gently. 'I've got Jessica, don't forget. Why don't you come round some time and meet her?'

Without taking her up on the suggestion, he asked, 'Did you stay on at the Infirmary after I left?'

'Yes. Until she was born. Afterwards I went nursing in the private sector, and eventually ended up here at the airport.'

'And do you like it?'

'Yes. I love it. The work is so varied. You never know who will walk into the centre and what they might have wrong with them.'

'Like me, for instance, having just wrestled with a knife man.'

She looked across at the strong wrist showing beneath the cuff of his shirt.

'I take it that the cut healed satisfactorily?'

'Mmm,' he said absently, and then surprised her by saying, 'So, when do you want me to call round at your place?'

Fabia laughed as happiness kindled inside her.

'Whenever our free times coincide. I only work weekday mornings so any afternoon or weekend will suit me.'

'I'm free on Saturday,' he replied. 'How about one o'clock?'

'Yes,' she said immediately. 'Come to lunch.'

'All right, I will,' he agreed slowly, as if he wasn't bubbling over at the prospect. 'I have your address somewhere.'

He wasn't going to tell her that he knew it off by heart and, feeling that he'd committed himself enough for one day, he got to his feet and held out his hand.

'Bye for now, Fabia.'

As she placed her hand in his she hoped that he couldn't feel her trembling. Hope was being born again. Bryce was back in her life. For how long she didn't know, but just the fact that he'd come in from the wilderness was enough to make her heart leap in her breast.

When he got home Bryce stripped off and went under the shower. He'd done a flight to Dallas, Texas, and after an overnight stay had just completed the return trip.

For the next twenty-four hours he was going to unwind, and before common sense asserted itself by reminding him that renewing his acquaintance with Fabia Ferguson would be like a turn of the knife every time he saw her, he quickly towelled himself dry and threw back the bed covers.

He'd sought her out again because he really had wanted to apologise, but he hadn't stuck to his original plan. A quick apology, followed by an even quicker departure had been his intention, and what had he done? Allowed himself to be invited into the home of the man who'd stolen his wife.

Although that wasn't strictly correct. From what Fabia had told him, she was no longer living in the smart house where she and Nick had started their married life. He supposed it was a cash problem. One small wage to keep both her and her child would have brought about the need for economy.

Her face came into his mind. The kind mouth, the beautiful violet eyes, long-lashed and clear, and the smooth golden swathe of her hair, fastened up while she was working.

Fabia had grace and style. It was amazing that

some guy hadn't made a play for her during the years since she'd been widowed. She even made his pulses quicken and there'd been few women who'd done that in recent years.

But maybe there was someone. She didn't have to divulge all her private life to him just because they'd met up again.

Fabia had been able to let go. She was the sensible one. He was the fool. Still grieving...still angry. Maybe if he'd had a child to cherish, like she had, it might have been different.

He hoped that her daughter wasn't a miniature version of the two sisters. The last thing he wanted was to be playing uncle to a small Tiffany.

What could he take her? A doll? A game? Sweets? And what for his hostess? He'd no ideas on that one. Though he knew one thing she wouldn't want him to bring...any more misery into her life. He would have to leave behind the great lump of bitterness that he carried around with him, otherwise he might shatter the tranquillity with which she'd surrounded herself.

CHAPTER TWO

BRYCE took Jessica a nurse's outfit and her mother flowers, and both recipients smiled their pleasure when he handed them over.

Especially the little girl who, he was relieved to see, looked more like her father than her mother…or her aunt.

'Are you related to us?' she'd asked when they'd opened the door to him, and he'd glanced at Fabia for guidance before replying. He'd no idea what she'd told her daughter about him, maybe nothing, but he hadn't wanted to dig any holes that he would have to climb out of at first meeting.

Yet did it matter? This would be the first and last time he would be socialising with his sister-in-law and her child. Being there was a gesture, nothing more.

'Bryce is your uncle,' Fabia said, patting her daughter's brown crown gently. 'Don't you remember me telling you, darling?'

'Mmm,' Jessica had said, and had moved on to the next question. 'Where are your wings? Mummy said that you fly.'

'It's the aeroplane that I'm in charge of that has the wings,' he'd said with a smile. 'I'm just the pilot.'

She was delightful, he thought enviously as he watched her, dressed in the nurse's outfit, spooning 'medicine' down her dolls. Here was a member of the opposite sex that he would love to spend some time

23

with. There would be no hurt or deceit to be had from this bubbly five-year-old.

'Lunch is ready,' Fabia called from the doorway, and as they went into a small raftered dining room overlooking a cottage garden bright with summer flowers, Bryce was surprised to find that he was enjoying himself.

'And so who looks after Jessica while you're at the airport?' he asked Fabia as they sat watching her play after the remains of the meal had been cleared away.

She smiled. 'I might have known that you'd ask that. You always were into basics.'

He grimaced but for once there was no bitterness in it as he remarked, 'Maybe that was where I fell short. Came over as boring.'

Her smiled broadened into laughter. 'Boring—you? Never. I've always thought of you as the most interesting person I've ever met.'

She turned her head away so that he wouldn't read what was in her eyes. He was also one of the most observant people she'd ever met, and although he'd never tuned into her feelings for him when Tiffany had been around, he might do now if she wasn't careful and this frail rapport between them was too precious to risk it being broken.

'My friend Maggie from next door looks after Jess in the mornings until it's time for school and, of course, I'm home in the afternoons.'

Bryce nodded. 'Sounds a reasonable enough arrangement.'

'So you approve?'

'I approve of everything I'm seeing and hearing,' he said with his eyes on her daughter, and Fabia wished that his glance had included herself. What would she have to do to make him notice her? Wear a mask so that she wouldn't be reminding him of Tiffany all the time?

He was still there in the early evening and, strangely reluctant to leave, Bryce suggested, 'How about me taking you both out to dinner, if it wouldn't be too late for Jessica? What time does she go to bed?'

'About half-eightish at weekends,' she told him.

'So we've got a couple of hours. How about it?'

'Yes,' she said slowly. 'That would be lovely. We don't go out all that much.'

Jessica had been listening and she said, 'Can I go in my nurse's dress...Uncle Bryce?'

'Yes, if it's all right with your mum.'

Fabia nodded and said in a low voice, 'The outfit was a stroke of genius. We'll be playing at hospitals for evermore.'

'Like old times, eh?'

'Yes, like old times,' she agreed wistfully.

But in the 'old times' that he had been referring to it had been the two of them who'd been the ones in the hospital set-up and they hadn't been playing. They'd worked in health care together and had loved it.

That time would never come again, with Bryce footloose and fancy-free up in the skies and herself down below, coping with her responsibilities.

'So where shall I take you to eat?' he asked with a glance at the village green across the way and the cluster of stone houses around it. 'You know this place better than I do.'

'There's a highly recommended restaurant a few

miles down the road that has a children's play area,' Fabia suggested.

'And would we be served without a reservation?'

'Yes, at this time. It gets busy later in the evening.'

'So, let's go,' he suggested, and was amazed that he could sound so upbeat about the idea.

They had no difficulty getting a table, and while they were waiting to be served Jessica played happily with other youngsters in a sandpit beside the restaurant gardens.

'So, are you happy with your lot?' Bryce found himself asking as Fabia observed her daughter fondly.

She turned her head at the question and as their glances held accepted that it wasn't going to be easy to answer. It depended on what degree of happiness he was referring to.

Yes, she was happy to have Jessica in her life. Yes, she was happy to still be in health care. Yes, she'd put the past behind her...up to a point. But she was still in love with the man beside her.

Having today discarded his smart pilot's uniform for casual wear, it hadn't lessened his attractions in her eyes—nothing would ever do that. She was so aware of him she couldn't believe he wasn't tuning into her longing.

But she'd had a lot of time to practise keeping her emotions under control, knowing that Jessica wouldn't thrive with a mother who was haunted by the sad past, and her answer when it came was proof of it.

'Yes. I am happy with my lot,' she said. 'I've had to work at it. Calmness of mind doesn't come easily after what we went through, as you are well aware.

But bitterness warps the mind, Bryce. Narrows the outlook. And is an uncomfortable bedfellow.'

'And that's one for me, is it?'

'Only you know if the cap fits.'

'You are obviously a kinder soul than I am.'

She shook her head.

'Rubbish! I've seen you on the wards and they don't come any more caring than that.'

He was almost smiling. Having a champion was something he wasn't used to. Especially one as attractive as this.

'You are determined to keep reminding me that I was once in medicine, aren't you? Do you disapprove of my change of career?'

'I don't disapprove, but I think it's a waste of your skills.'

'Have you any idea how much time and money it cost me to train as a pilot?'

'No.'

'I had no change out of sixty thousand pounds and I have spent years with my nose to the grindstone getting to where I am now. The initial training took all the money I made from the house sale. I'm affluent enough now but I wasn't then.'

'And doing that helped you to forget?'

'No. It didn't.'

'It's never too late to start putting the past behind you.'

'With you in front of me? Tiffany's sister?'

'I can't help what I look like,' she said levelly, 'and don't start that again, Bryce. My life hasn't exactly been easy since I was left on my own, but I don't go round with a great big chip on my shoulder.'

This is awful, she thought as soon as the words

were out. One moment we're at peace with each other…and the next…

'I'm sorry, Fabia,' he said tightly. 'I deserved that and it's the reason I'm here…because of how I was with you then.' He reached across and took her hand, squeezing it gently. 'Will you forgive me for putting my usual blight on the day?'

Her face was brightening. 'Yes, of course.'

The touch of his fingers was like balm to her soul and the look in his eyes said that he wasn't unmoved by the contact either.

She would forgive him anything…because she loved him and ached to see him so miserable. If he would give her the chance, she would try to make him happy again.

At that moment the waitress appeared with the food and Fabia called Jessica across to her.

'I think we'd better wash your hands before you eat,' she said, and the child pulled a face.

'They're not dirty,' she protested, and the waitress smiled.

'Go and do as Mummy says,' she urged. 'Daddy will wait for you, won't you?' she said to Bryce.

Fabia thought, Oh dear!

'Of course,' he said smoothly, before Jessica had time to start pointing out 'relative' issues and, holding her mother's hand, she skipped off obediently.

Jessica went back to the sandpit after they'd eaten, and Fabia and Bryce took their coffee into the restaurant garden to be near her. Suddenly there was a cry from inside. 'Is there a doctor anywhere on the premises?'

They were both on their feet in a flash, but he put a restraining hand on her arm.

'I'll see what's wrong,' he told her. 'Stay here with Jessica. She might wander off.' He hurried inside.

'I'm a doctor,' he told the agitated manager. 'What's the problem?'

'Customer collapsed in the bar area,' he said. 'Looks serious.'

As soon as Bryce saw the victim he knew that it was indeed serious. He'd seen it countless times before—cardiac arrest. The bluey-grey look around the mouth, the total unconsciousness.

'Phone for an ambulance. Tell them it's a heart attack,' he said urgently as he knelt beside the victim.

He put his ear to the man's chest and there was no heartbeat, no pulse at wrist or neck. He had to try to get him breathing again or there could be brain damage, or even death.

After he'd loosened the man's shirt collar, he prised his mouth open to check that there was nothing blocking the airway and then listened once more for any signs of breathing, such as air from the mouth or the rise and fall of his chest but there was nothing.

At that moment he heard Fabia's voice telling those who were crowding around, 'Stand back, please. Give the patient some air and the doctor some space.'

When he looked up she said in answer to the question in his eyes, 'Jessica's with the waitress.'

He nodded and as she knelt beside him he placed his lips over the victim's mouth and breathed deeply into him. He repeated the action a few times but there was still no response and they eyed each other sombrely.

'Take over,' he said, and started to press down with

both hands crossed on the lower part of the breast-bone but clear of the ribs, while Fabia continued the mouth-to-mouth resuscitation on a basis of one breath to every five compressions.

Suddenly, miraculously, as the sirens of an ambulance sounded on the evening air, there were signs of life. The man was breathing again, and as paramedics came hurrying in with their equipment Fabia and Bryce stepped back to let them take over.

'Well done, Dr Hollister,' she said softly as the man was stretchered out to the waiting ambulance. 'Now, that really was like old times...the good old times.'

Bryce was smiling. 'Yes. There's nothing to equal the feeling of being there in a life-threatening situation when one is needed.'

'What do you think his chances are?' she asked, with the wonder of the moment still upon her.

'Hard to say, but certainly better than when we first saw him.' He took her arm and led her back towards the dining room. 'Let's go and find Jessica.'

They found her bandaging the waitress's arm. When she saw them she lifted up her face and said protestingly, 'I'm the nurse today, Mummy. You should have sent for me.'

As Bryce turned away to hide a smile, Fabia told her, 'I know you are. Next time there is an emergency we'll remember to fetch you, won't we...Bryce?'

'Yes, absolutely,' he agreed solemnly, and as the young protester yawned he added, 'I think that it is somebody's bedtime. I'll settle the bill and then shall we go?'

Fabia nodded. Yet there was regret in her. Soon the day would be over and she doubted whether there would be others. It's just a one-off, she told herself. Don't get your hopes up. Bryce will probably drop you both off at the door and that will be it. In any case, how do you know that he hasn't got something planned for later? It's only half past eight.

He didn't drop them off at the door. He sat and read the newspaper while Fabia got Jessica ready for bed, and once she was settled and Fabia came back downstairs he said, 'And so what are you doing for the rest of your weekend?'

'Nothing much,' she told him. 'Household chores, and I usually take Jessica to the park on Sundays. What about you?'

'I've got two long hauls coming up so that will be me sorted, for a while.'

'Yes, I see,' she said quietly.

This was going to be it, she could feel it in her bones, and when he got to his feet she knew she wasn't wrong.

'Thanks for lunch, Fabia,' he said gravely, 'and for letting me meet your daughter. She's a charmer. I was going to say that you're a lucky woman, but it's not strictly true, is it?'

She reached out and touched his cheek gently.

'Life is what we make it, Bryce. Take care while you're up there in the skies, and when you're down below, too. Jessica hasn't said much about meeting you today, but tomorrow she'll be full of it.'

'And what about you?' he asked with the gravity still upon him.

'I'll be remembering it, too,' she told him with a smile. 'Every moment of it.'

'Really? Then you're not as much like Tiffany as I keep thinking you are.'

'You always knew that,' she told him levelly. 'We might have been sisters, Bryce, and I might look very much like her. That is something I can't help. But don't tar me with the same brush. It isn't fair.'

His face had the tight look again that she dreaded.

'You're quite right. It wasn't fair of me at all. Forgive me. Whatever else I may be, I'm honest, and when I told you that it was good to be back working with you tonight, I meant it. But it's not going to bring me down from the skies. Goodnight, Fabia.'

As she watched him stride out to his car, Fabia's mind was in a whirl. He was like a chameleon—one moment his old self, the next the cold stranger carrying his bitterness around with him like a destructive cell. Yet there had been moments today when she'd been totally happy.

She'd never expected there to be anything between them right from the moment she'd realised she was in love with him all those years ago. For even if he hadn't been so obsessed with her sister, too many people would have been hurt if anything had come of it.

Yet the same morality hadn't bothered the other two, Tiffany and Nick. When they'd begun their affair they'd had no consideration for herself and Bryce.

And now, even though his wife was long gone, Bryce was still obsessed with her, so that he wasn't going to look at another woman, least of all herself.

But there'd been something about today that had been special. He'd loved Jessica, for one thing, been really interested in their lives…and had taken them out to dine.

And treating the heart attack victim together and bringing him back to life had created a euphoria in

her that she hadn't felt for a long time. Surely he
wasn't going to walk away from them after all that.

Bryce was in a thoughtful mood as he drove home.
There had been moments during the day when he'd
felt completely at ease with Fabia, just as it had been
in the old days, and it had got to him. And the child,
Jessica, had been enchanting.

Then there'd been that business with the heart attack victim that had made him feel nostalgic, but not
so much that he was going to abandon flying.

He'd always wanted to fly, but medicine had come
first until his private life had fallen apart and he'd
decided that everything had to change if he was to
stay sane.

But now, by a strange coincidence, he'd met someone from the past—the other victim—and she was
making him feel ashamed of his bleakness of spirit.

Fabia Ferguson was a woman to be admired. She'd
been there with him all day, serene in her golden fairness, and he'd been amazed that there wasn't a new
man in her life as she wasn't carrying the memory of
a faithless partner around with her like he was.

And so what had he done? Allowed himself to become vulnerable. A state of mind that he'd vowed
never to be in again. He'd expected the atmosphere
to be pleasantly polite, but he'd fitted into their home
and surroundings like a glove and knew that if the
opportunity arose he would go back. If only to see
little Jessica. He wasn't going to admit that her
mother had anything to do with how he felt, although
he had looked at her a couple of times without thinking of Tiffany and something long dead had stirred
in him when he'd held her hand.

*   *   *

A week had gone by with no word from Bryce and Fabia was telling herself again that she hadn't been wrong. He was backing off. After letting himself get involved in her life, he was retreating. He would have had to have been at the airport some time during the week, but there had been no head-turning, dark-uniformed figure appearing out of the blue.

Giles Grainger had been thinking that she had seemed more approachable of late, but his top nurse had gone back into her shell and he felt, as he had so many times before, that the unattached members of his sex must be blind if they couldn't see what lay beneath their noses. Yet, he thought whimsically, maybe they did see, but received so little encouragement they didn't do anything about it.

The school summer holidays were due to start and once that happened the airport would be busier than usual, which meant the unit would be, too.

There would be no time for concerning himself about the private lives of his staff once the general public arrived with their aches and pains, which were sometimes imagined, sometimes minor and on other occasions dire emergencies.

They had to cope with them all. Diabetic comas, suspected blood clots after flights, nausea, caused either by nerves or excitement, and people who had only just been discharged from hospital as in-patients and were risking flying almost immediately while they were still in a delicate state. Pregnant mothers were also sometimes visitors to the walk-in centre, feeling ill after flights, or before them.

In many instances all the patient needed was re-assurance, and the calm competence of his staff always guaranteed that, but there was always the chance that something really was wrong.

On the Friday of that same week Fabia was faced with a patient with an unexpected problem. A man walked into the centre covered in what appeared to be watery blisters.

'I've been off colour for a few days,' he told her, then pointed to the rash. 'Woke up with these all over me this morning and they itch like crazy. The wife says they look the same as when the children had chickenpox, and as my GP's surgery will be closed for the weekend by the time I get home, I thought I'd see what you people had to say.'

As she examined him Fabia thought that his wife was right. It was the chickenpox rash he'd got, but from where?

'How long is it since your children had the illness?' she asked.

'Oh, it was years ago.'

'Have you been in contact with anyone who's got it at the moment?'

'Not that I know of.'

'Well, you've picked it up somewhere. Are you flying out or in?'

'In. We've just come back from Majorca.'

'Good.'

'Why good?'

'Well, for one thing it won't have spoiled your holiday, as an adult with the virus often feels much more poorly than a child who's got it. So it's preferable that you are treated for it in this country if you should have any complications.

'If you do have any problems when you get home, phone your GP's after-hours service and be guided by what they advise. In the meantime, take paracetamol. Your temperature is a bit high.'

'Yes, I know. I've been burning up all the time we've been airborne,' he said.

'So take care and do as I've said if you feel any worse. And whatever you do, don't scratch the tops off the spots or they will leave scars.'

He nodded.

'There'll be some leg pulling when the wife hears about this.'

'Just tell her to be thankful that it's not her who has chickenpox.'

'Aye,' he said gloomily, and went.

When Fabia was almost on the point of leaving for home, a message came through to say that a woman was about to give birth on a plane that had just landed from Dallas, Fort Worth, and that help was needed.

'The pilot is in charge,' Giles was told.

He asked in amazement, 'Of what? The aircraft or the delivery?'

He was informed with a chuckle, 'Both.'

'The crew are doing what they can,' he told Fabia as she prepared to go to them, 'but they need paramedics and a couple of nurses. You're the only one available at the moment, but when one of the others is free, I'll send her along.'

'Gate twenty-seven,' he called after her as she whizzed out of the glass doors and into the throbbing terminal.

Every time he'd been through the airport that week Bryce had avoided the walk-in centre. It would have been so easy to have gone in there and resumed communications between Fabia and himself, but he hadn't done it.

He felt he was on the brink of something that he might not be able to cope with. Fabia was too much in his thoughts. Her smile, the way she moved, the clear gaze that held no rancour.

He'd enjoyed the previous Saturday more than he wanted to admit, and it would have been so simple to go on from there. But did he want to be squirming all the time as he observed her generosity of spirit, when he was so far from attaining the same kind of acceptance?

There was no need for him to be on a guilt trip, he kept telling himself firmly. He'd done nothing wrong…except let bitterness take such a hold on him that it had warped his outlook.

He'd felt aggrieved for so long, he wouldn't know how to cope without the lump of misery inside him, he'd gone on to tell himself. It would be like casting aside an old friend if he suddenly started to feel happy.

But he was no fool. Of late it had become even more apparent that the only good thing in his life was his job, and what a wash-out that made him appear.

When the purser came to him during the last leg of the regular flight from Dallas to say that a pregnant passenger was about to give birth he rolled his eyes heavenwards.

'Is she sure?' he asked crisply.

'Yes. Very sure. The contractions are fast and regular.'

'Have any of you dealt with a delivery before?' he asked.

His co-pilot shuddered and begged, 'Leave me out of it. I can't stand the sight of blood.'

'Not the real thing,' the purser told him, 'but we know the routine. The problem is that it's twins and if they arrive now they'll be premature.'

Bryce whistled softly.

'Can she hang on until we land?'

'It's doubtful.'

'Take over,' he told the co-pilot and went to where some of the first-class passengers had vacated their seats to give the woman room to lie down and the staff space to attend her.

'Don't worry, Anna. I'm a doctor, as well as a pilot,' he told her as she gazed up at him apprehensively. 'Now, you're going to be just fine. We shall be landing in a few minutes and the medical staff of the airport will be waiting for us.

'They will have sent for an ambulance so, you see, there's no need to be afraid...and if your little ones won't wait that long, I'll take over.'

'But were you an obstetrician?' the husband asked frantically.

'I have worked in obstetrics,' Bryce told him calmly, 'although I was in coronary care when I left the NHS.'

As his wife was gripped by another contraction the man said, 'Thank goodness for that.'

As they touched down the head of one of the babies appeared and Bryce cried to the mother. 'Push now! Hard!'

In the background he could hear the cabin crew telling passengers to keep their seat belts fastened to avoid congestion as the airport nurse came aboard.

The perspiring mother was doing as she was told

and with one last final shuddering groan the baby was there, a wrinkled, red-looking little mortal who didn't need any pat on the back to bring air into her lungs. She was already howling lustily, almost as if in protest at the indignity of her entry into the world.

As the purser held out a blanket, which was all they had to wrap her in, a voice from beside him said, 'This is getting to be a habit, Bryce. Give her to me.' When he looked up, Fabia was there, holding out a clean white towel.

'Sure thing,' he agreed as the feeling of inevitability that had gripped him of late surfaced once more. 'Just as soon as I've clamped the cord. And brace yourself, Fabia. There's another one to come.'

'What?' she gasped, and whispered in his ear, 'Poor mother! Poor babies!'

'What about poor me?' he asked quizzically as he bent to the task. 'I've just flown in from Dallas! This is the second time in just over a week that you and I have been in this sort of situation…a medical emergency. Do you think that someone up there is trying to tell me something?'

She didn't get the chance to answer. Anna cried out, 'I'm going to have to push again.' And at that moment her anxious husband keeled over.

The cabin staff rushed forward and lifted him onto a nearby seat while Fabia and Bryce concentrated on the imminent birth. It was quick and normal like the first one, and as Bryce picked up a tiny boy he said, 'Any more towels where that came from?'

'Just one,' she told him with a smile. 'If there are any others to come, you'll have to take off your nice white shirt.'

He pulled a face.

'Not after I've had it on for the last eight hours. But, no, we're stopping at two, aren't we?' he said with a smile for the exhausted mother.

When the second baby began to exercise his vocal cords in tune with his sister a cheer went up from the passengers. As Bryce grinned across at the golden-haired nurse beside him in triumphant satisfaction she thought wistfully that it was like that night in the restaurant. This was the man she knew...and loved.

While Bryce was clamping the cord of the second arrival from its placenta, footsteps on the metal walk-way outside indicated that the emergency services had arrived.

When two paramedics appeared, a passenger called to them, 'You're too late, chaps. The pilot and the nurse have done your job for you.'

Bryce looked down at the delighted mother with a child on each arm and told them, 'The placenta hasn't come away yet. She has a heart condition, which we didn't have time to delve into, but hasn't needed ox-ygen so far.'

Pointing to the husband, who was coming round, he told them, 'That's the proud father. It was all too much for him, I'm afraid, having his children born on a jumbo jet with a captive audience.'

The paramedic in charge nodded and, turning to the trainee ambulance technician who'd come with him, said, 'Let's get these folks to hospital.' With a smile for the passengers he added, 'And then you can be on your way.'

'It was wonderful. I wouldn't have missed it for the world,' a woman sitting nearby said, and those around her were in full agreement.

*   *   *

As Fabia and Bryce entered the terminal building he said casually, 'After no contact for all that time, now we seemed fated to meet, don't we? How are you and the enchanting Jessica?'

'Fine,' she said, 'and with regards to that young lady I should have been off duty an hour ago. I'm going to have to move. The last thing I want is for Jessica to find me not there when school comes out.'

'Absolutely,' he agreed. 'More precious than gold, aren't they? What about those two tiny mites, eh? Making their appearance under such circumstances! I thought I might have forgotten the routine, but it's surprising how soon it all comes back.'

'You were fantastic,' she said softly. 'But, then, you always were a joy to work with.'

'Was I?'

She could have told him that it hadn't just been on the wards she'd thought that. It had been every time and everywhere she'd been near him. She'd never dreamt that a time might come when she could tell him the whole truth of it.

But it hadn't, had it? Bryce was just as out of reach now as he'd been then. Tiffany was dead, but nothing had changed. She was still there as far as he was concerned. Like a silent reminder of all that was past.

Outside the walk-in centre he said, 'We'll have to get together again some time, Fabia.'

'I'd like that,' she told him simply.

'Good. I'll be in touch. Bye for now.' And with a brief wave of the hand he was gone.

CHAPTER THREE

WHEN Bryce opened the door of the smart detached house that he'd bought only recently, after returning to the area, he frowned as he was met by a hollow feeling of emptiness.

He'd noticed it a few times of late and was vaguely irritated by it. It had never been there before he'd met up with Fabia and her daughter and he'd thought that the subdued sort of contentment he'd striven for wasn't as satisfying to come home to as it had been.

And now today they'd met again, on familiar territory in more ways than one, and he'd told Fabia that he would be in touch. In other words, he'd admitted that he'd like to see her again.

The truth of it was that the moment he'd seen the flash of bright blue uniform out of the corner of his eye and had looked up to see her standing there, calmly holding out the towel, he'd known just how much he really did want to see her again.

If it brought back bad memories, so be it. As she'd so rightly said, Fabia couldn't help who she looked like and they *were* the victims rather than the perpetrators.

They and Jessica were also all that was left of the two families so it was understandable that he couldn't keep up the pretence of ignoring her presence at the airport. Not when every time he saw her he realised her worth.

Her calm reasoning and acceptance of her lot had

irritated him at first, but the more he thought about her, the more he felt that he had something to learn from Fabia.

She'd said that they didn't get out a lot, she and Jessica. Not asking for sympathy, merely stating a fact. Maybe he could do something about that, he thought as he showered and changed. Take them out for the day perhaps, to a theme park, or the zoo, or for a sail along one of the town's many waterways.

Steady on! he told himself. Don't get carried away. Nothing has changed. Fabia is still Tiffany's sister.

Yet it didn't stop him from calling in at the walk-in centre the next time he was at the airport. He caught Fabia coming out of one of the small surgeries at the rear of the building and the look on her face when she saw him made his collar suddenly feel too tight.

'Hi, there,' he said casually. 'Are you free?'

She shook her head.

'No. Not at the moment. I've got a very fretful toddler in there who could have a convulsion if his temperature doesn't come down soon.'

'Oh, dear! I'll ring you tonight, then. Will you be in?'

She smiled. 'Yes. You can always count on that. Jess goes to bed about seven and after that the evening is my own.'

'Suppose I ring before then, so that I can have a word with her, too?'

'Yes, of course. She keeps asking when she'll see you again as we're very short on family. Plenty of friends but no kith and kin.' With a quick backward glance she added, 'I have to get back to my patient, Bryce.'

He nodded.

'Until tonight, then. Bye, Fabia.'

Driving home, Bryce thought ruefully that he always seemed to talk to her in staccato sentences. Yet he was the most articulate of men. Or at least he had been once.

Her comment about shortage of family members hadn't gone unnoticed. The same applied to him. Both their parents were dead. He'd been an only son and there'd been just Fabia and Tiffany in their family, so it was only to be expected that she must sometimes feel very alone.

Maybe that was why she was always so pleased to see him…she was lonely. Or perhaps it was for old times' sake. He doubted whether it was for any other reason.

When he made the promised phone call that evening, Jessica's voice spoke in his ear.

'Is that you, Uncle Bryce?' she asked before he'd time to speak.

'No. It's Father Christmas,' he told her in a gruff playtime sort of voice, which brought forth squeals of laughter and the comment that it couldn't be as it wasn't snowing.

'So, what have you been doing at school today?' he asked.

'Not much. It was the last day before the holidays,' he was told. 'I'm in a new class when I go back.'

'And so what are you going to do while you're on holiday.'

'I'll be with Maggie and her boys in the mornings and with Mummy in the afternoons.'

'Are you going away?'

He was aware that he was asking Jessica questions that he ought to be asking her mother, and when she said in a more subdued voice, 'I don't know,' and then surprised him by asking 'Are you?' Bryce thought that he was hoist with his own petard.

'I might,' he said. 'I have a little house in Cornwall.'

'Is that why Mummy said you're a Cornishman?' she wanted to know.

'It could be.'

He'd almost decided to go back there permanently when Tiffany had died, but the urge to fly had changed all that. He'd wanted to be in the thick of it, where the pulse beat faster.

But he did still have his parents' cottage in St Ives, and whenever he went back the magic of the winding streets with their pretty colour-washed houses and the mighty Atlantic surging in on golden beaches, was like balm to his battered pride.

When Fabia came on the line she was laughing.

'Are you what?' she questioned. 'What was Jessica asking you about?'

'She wanted to know if I was going away on holiday. I asked her first, though.'

There was silence for a moment and then she said, 'We haven't got anything planned. I'm taking two weeks' leave and the rest of the time it will be Jess spending the mornings with Maggie until I get home.'

'I've still got my mum and dad's house in St Ives,' he said slowly, as if someone was pulling his strings. 'You can stay there for the two weeks that you're off if you want.'

There was an even longer silence this time, until at last he asked, 'Fabia, are you still there?'

'Yes, I'm still here,' she replied. 'I'm just trying to work out why you should offer. You know, Bryce, I'm not a charity case.'

'I never thought you were. It was just that the place is empty. It needs living in and I wasn't intending going down there until September. Think about it, Fabia. The offer's there.'

'Thanks. I will,' she said briefly. 'What was it that you wanted me for this morning at the airport?'

'Ah, yes, that. I was wondering if you'd like to go out somewhere for the day some time. It would give me the chance to see some more of your delightful daughter.'

'Even though I'll be part of the package?' she asked, with the feeling that she came a poor second to Jessica.

'Of course,' he said quickly. 'Whatever do you mean by that?'

He knew very well why she'd asked. She sensed that the barriers were still up. That he still thought of her as Tiffany's sister. Yet would he be asking her out if that was the case?

Yes. He would. He was being pulled two ways. Part of him wanted to stay clear of any involvement with Fabia and the rest of him was eager to be with the serene woman that he'd once worked with in health care.

But the look in her eyes that morning hadn't been the forerunner to this, he thought. She'd already said that she didn't want charity and now was casting doubts on just how much he wanted her along on any outing with Jessica.

Suddenly it was imperative to let her see that wasn't the case. He'd thought that asking them out would have made that clear, but it seemed that Fabia needed to know that he really did want to be with her.

So he said in a softer tone, 'I know what you're thinking and it's not true any more. I accept you for who you are, and what you are. Whether you can accept me on those same terms I don't know, as I'm not the man I used to be. Although I'm working on it.'

'I accept you on any terms, Bryce,' she said in a low voice. 'Yes, we'd love to spend the day with you.'

'Great! So where shall we go and when?'

'Any day next week would suit me, depending on what flights you're on—you choose.'

'All right. I have a couple of days free mid-week. How about Wednesday?'

'Yes. Wednesday will be fine.'

'Then I'll pick you up around tennish,' he said, and with the feeling that they'd said enough for the time being he didn't prolong the conversation.

Chatsworth House, in the golden rays of a summer sun, stood in magnificence behind a sparkling lake as Bryce drove into one of the parking areas created to accommodate the influx of visitors to the stately home.

It was only eleven o'clock and already the grounds were filling up with eager sightseers, bound for the lakeside, the adventure playground, the farmyard or one of the eateries.

When he'd called to pick them up and had suggested this place, Fabia had observed him doubtfully. He'd asked her, 'You don't think it's a good idea?'

'The answer to that is yes and no,' she'd told him. 'Yes, because Jess will love the animals and the adventure playground. No, because we once went there as a foursome, Nick and I and Tiffany and you. If it brings back bad memories, it will put you off for the rest of the day. Had you forgotten?'

He'd observed her steadily. 'No. I hadn't forgotten…and I'm not going to let it throw me. The four of us went to a lot of places together and if I start picking and choosing because of that, we could end up going nowhere. So, what do you say?'

She'd smiled. 'I say…let's go, then.'

And now here they were. In the grounds of one of Derbyshire's finest houses with a warm summer day ahead of them and Jessica straining at the leash to get to the animals.

The brief soul-searching that had gone on before they'd left had been a forerunner to a friendly and relaxed atmosphere, and as the car had sped along, with Jessica and herself in the back seat, Fabia had been smiling at the thought of the day ahead.

At one point, when Bryce had been telling her about a recent flight where he'd had a passenger from hell on board, he'd commented mildly. 'It wasn't anything to smile at, Fabia.'

She'd eyed him apologetically. 'I'm sorry. I know it wasn't. It's just that it's so lovely to be out and about I can't help smiling.'

It hadn't been the right moment to tell him that he was the cause of her happiness, being with him, near him and knowing that it was his idea they should spend the day together.

When Jessica saw the animals in the farmyard her face lit up. In the different pens there were sheep, goats, donkeys, rabbits, chickens and pheasants, and nearby were fish tanks full of young trout which the children were allowed to feed.

As she joined the eager throng, with Fabia and Bryce standing nearby, he said casually, 'She looks more like Nick than you, doesn't she?'

'Mmm,' she murmured, wondering what was coming next.

'Does that bother you?'

'No, of course not. He was her father after all. It's only natural she should resemble him.'

'He never saw her, did he?'

'No. Jess was born eight months after he died. But why are we going down that road? I thought you'd decided that the past was past.'

He took her hand in his and gave it a quick squeeze.

'Sorry. It's just that my mind has been so full of the two of you, the fact that Nick had something to do with Jessica being around had barely registered. He paid a high price for what he did, didn't he?'

'Yes, he did,' she replied steadily. 'And in case it has escaped your attention, I was never given the chance to see if he would have wanted to come back to me once he knew I was pregnant.'

'Wha-at?' There was disbelief in the bright blue gaze holding hers. 'You would have had him back.'

'I didn't say that,' she told him flatly. 'I said that I never had the chance to find out if he would have wanted to *come* back. And now can we change the subject?'

'Mummy! Uncle Bryce!' Jessica was calling. 'Can I hold one of the rabbits?'

'Yes,' she told her, glad of the diversion. 'Children are allowed to hold some of the smaller animals.'

As they went across to watch her stroke a tiny black rabbit, Bryce said contritely, 'You must think I put the dampener on everything.'

She shook her head and the long golden swathe of her hair glinted in the summer sun.

'No, I don't. I just wish I could take some of your hurt away.'

He smiled. 'You already have.'

'I have! How?'

'Just by being here. Being yourself.'

Fabia felt tears clutch at her throat. There was so much more she would like to be to him. She would like to wake up next to him each morning. Hold him in her arms through the night. Kiss away the dark moments that still came over him.

But the voice of caution was forever whispering in her ear, telling her that what little progress they were making could be wiped out if she were to tell Bryce how much she loved him.

Be satisfied with what you've got, it told her. At least he isn't always comparing you with Tiffany now. Hopefully he *is* seeing you as the person you are and not as a clone of your sister.

The adventure playground had been erected in the woods beside the grand house. It was one of the finest of its kind in the country, and Bryce's smile was young and carefree as he chaperoned Jessica on the climbing frames and watched over her as she went on the swings and came down the slides.

Fabia felt tears swell up again. He should be doing this with children of his own, she thought sadly.

But blissfully he didn't see it like that. Apart from

those few depressing comments about Nick earlier, he was totally enchanted by Jessica and she thought that maybe this was a sort of justice. That he was here to play with Nick's daughter.

They lunched in The Carriage House restaurant, and once the meal was over they took Jessica to watch the dairy herd being milked at half past three. And all the time the sun beamed down out of a cloudless sky.

Overcome by her exertions and the fresh air, the little girl fell asleep on the way home and had to be roused when they reached the outskirts of the village.

As Bryce carried her inside Fabia said, 'Jess will be out like a light again as soon as she's had a glass of milk and a biscuit. If you'd like to hang on, I'll make us a sandwich.'

'Sure,' he agreed easily, as he deposited one sleepy child on to the sofa.

Her heartbeat quickened. She would have him to herself for a little while.

Once Jessica was in bed she went into the kitchen to make the promised snack. As she sliced fresh bread at the worktop and covered it with cheese and pickles, Fabia wasn't aware that he'd followed her and was standing a couple of paces behind her. Picking up the kettle, she swung round to take it to the tap and found herself up against the hard wall of Bryce's chest.

At the look in his eyes she became still and, with the kettle hanging limply from her hand, watched, mesmerised, as his arms reached out for her.

Bryce had touched her before. A squeeze of the hand, a hold of the arm, but it had been nothing like this. The second that his arms were around her she was on fire. Like a thirsty traveller at an oasis, she was drinking in the magic of the moment as if in fear that it might be a mirage.

But it was no mirage. When his mouth came down onto hers, Fabia gave herself up to the moment with a desperate abandon born of years of deprivation. She'd always known it would be like this, she thought exultantly as her breasts quickened against him and her thighs ached with the age-old longing.

It wasn't just Bryce's skill and integrity she'd fallen in love with all that time ago. His dark charisma had attracted her, too, and now, unbelievably, passion was sweeping away all their defences. Passion newly born. But even as she was revelling in the wonder of it he was putting her away from him with a groan.

'You're regretting letting the bond between us take over, aren't you?' she cried. 'How could you kiss me like that and not mean it? It's still Tiffany, isn't it? Have you never made love to anyone else since she died?'

He shook his head bleakly.

'No. And what do I do? Let down my guard with you of all people.'

'Thanks for making it sound so romantic!' she said, violet eyes sparking. 'I've never been with anyone else either, so doesn't that tell you something?'

'Oh, yes,' he agreed sombrely. 'It tells me that we're a pair of fools for putting our lives on hold like we have.'

'Speak for yourself,' she rapped back. 'The only reason I've been celibate is because I've been in love for years with a man who doesn't love me. It's nothing to do with Nick. I've not been carrying around a great big chip on my shoulder like you have.'

His face was grim in the summer twilight. 'Is that

so? Well, whoever the fellow is, he's a fool. That's all I have to say to that. If it wasn't for the past, we might have—'

'Stop talking about the past,' she said in quiet anger, aware of the sleeping child upstairs. 'Go home to your memories. I hope they keep you warm.'

'Now you're talking stupid,' he said in a low voice of his own, 'but I will go home.'

'Good!' she cried, and, picking up one of the sandwiches that she'd just made, she slapped it into his hand, telling him icily, 'That will help you to get your strength back after all that wasted exertion.'

To her absolute amazement he began to laugh, and that was the final straw.

'I've only served up a cheese sandwich,' she flared, 'but you—you have served up humiliation, and now you're following it up with mockery.'

He held out a placatory hand but she pushed it away and, opening the back door, stood waiting for him to leave.

'The next time you feel like handing out charity, look for someone else,' she told him stonily.

'I told you the other day that asking you out had nothing to do with that.'

'I'm not talking about going to Chatsworth,' she flung back at him. 'I was referring to what's just happened here.'

Bryce paused in the doorway.

'That wasn't charity either, Fabia,' he said tonelessly. 'It was need…on both our parts.'

When he'd gone Fabia sank down onto the nearest chair and gazed bleakly into space. If she didn't love him so much his reaction wouldn't have mattered, but stupidly she'd thought that this was it, Bryce was finally seeing her as she wanted him to.

Those brief passionate moments had been like paradise on earth and then he'd spoiled it with that sepulchral groan that had had a message all of its own.

And what had she done then? Blurted out that she was in love with a man who didn't love her. And Bryce had patronised her by saying that if they hadn't once been related, he might have considered something more positive between them.

All right, he hadn't said it in so many words, but that was what he'd been about to pronounce. How was she ever going to face him again? And was Bryce so dumb that it hadn't occurred to him that he might be the unknown loved one?

'Dumb' wasn't the right word. Maybe 'numb' was a better one. And if that was the case, it was time he snapped out of it. But did any of it matter? She couldn't see any future fraternising on his part, not after what had just happened.

So Fabia was in love and the jerk didn't return her feelings, Bryce thought as he drove home. The fellow must be insane, or else he was already married and she wasn't the type to break up a marriage, not Fabia. Not she who knew all about the pain of such goings-on.

Yet, considering she was in love with someone else, she'd been a joyous creature in his arms. Uninhibited, passionate, offering herself like a woman truly in love.

Oh, hell! Was she in love with him? he wondered raggedly as he pulled over to the side of the road.

She'd said it was someone she'd known for years. She'd known him for years.

It couldn't be so. Never by word or deed had she ever given him cause to think that before. But there'd been the look on her face the other day when he'd called in at the centre…and tonight as she'd swung round to fill the kettle.

You're mistaken, he told himself firmly. Fabia's not in love with you. You have too high an opinion of yourself. Yet, having told himself he was wrong, he had a lurking feeling of disappointment. Wasn't he just the least bit in love with her?

As the thoughts kept going round in his mind Bryce drove on. He admitted that he and she were at a stage where he wanted to keep seeing her, but was it because he was lonely, or because he was captivated by little Jessica, or for some other reason that lay deep in his subconscious?

By the time Fabia presented herself at the walk-in centre the next morning, she had put all thoughts of the previous night's happenings out of her head. Or thought she had until Bryce walked in with an armful of red roses and brought a like colour to her cheeks.

It was at a moment when she was actually free and the other nurse on duty wasn't so, apart from the student on Reception, they had the place to themselves.

'I thought you were off today,' she said in confusion when she saw him.

'I am,' he told her in a low voice, 'but I wanted to bring you these by way of an apology. I was an insensitive oaf last night and I'm sorry.'

'So am I,' she told him. 'I'm sorry I made such a fuss.'

He smiled. 'No. You were wonderful. This guy you're in love with doesn't know what he's missing. Is it anyone I know? You said you'd known him for years.'

He was watching her expression to see if it gave anything away, but Fabia was on her guard this morning and her face was serene as she replied, 'No. It's no one that you know, Bryce, and I feel stupid for mentioning him. It's not a big passion, more like something that causes the odd pang now and then.'

'I see.'

If he'd wanted to say anything else that was relative, he didn't get a chance. A man had just come through the door, limping badly, and when he saw Fabia he said weakly, 'It feels as if my toes are crushed. Some clown with a luggage trolley ran over my foot.'

She flashed Bryce an apologetic smile and he turned to go, 'I'll see you around,' he said casually.

'Mmm,' she murmured, adding in a low voice, 'Thanks for the flowers. They're lovely.'

Her heart was beating faster, her pulses quickening. The last thing she'd ever have expected was that he would bring her flowers. It made her feel special somehow. As if for once he wasn't seeing her as good old Fabia.

If just for once he'd seen her as a slender blonde with violet eyes and a kind mouth she would be happy.

As the latest visitor to the walk-in centre took off a flattened-looking trainer and a smelly sock, Fabia examined his toes with a practised eye.

They did look crushed. The soft plastic shoe had

provided little protection from the wheels of the trolley and the foot was already beginning to swell.

'I'm going to bathe your foot and then put a cold compress on it,' she told him. 'It's good for reducing the swelling, but I do feel that you need to go to A and E to have it looked at. Especially the little toe. I feel there could be a fracture there.'

He was eyeing her gloomily.

'Good start to the holiday this is. Can't I wait until I get there.'

'Not really. As the injury happened before you left the country it needs to be dealt with here, otherwise you may have to pay for treatment privately while you're abroad.'

When he'd gone hobbling off, Fabia picked up the flowers. She was wishing that Bryce had brought them as a man in love, rather than as an apology. But she told herself to be thankful to have him in her life again. He might disappear out of it any day and then she would be back to the emptiness of an existence without him once more.

It had been clear that he hadn't forgotten her telling him she was in love with someone else, and surprisingly he'd been curious, which was a mild description of how he would have been if he'd known that it was him that she loved.

If he had been anyone else but Tiffany's husband, she would take her chances and tell him how she felt. But it was too big a risk to take.

Bryce would think she was as immoral as her sister if he discovered that she'd been in love with him while he and Tiffany had been married.

What a sad can of worms had been opened on the

day that Nick had tried to overtake on the motorway with such disastrous consequences for them all.

Out of the whole sorry mess Bryce had been the only one who was blameless. Her own husband and his wife had been planning to go away together and she…she had been in love with her brother-in-law for years.

It had happened when they'd begun working together in health care and she'd had the chance to see the depth of him, the integrity and dedication that had made him one of the top doctors at the big hospital that served the town where they lived.

Previously she'd only met him socially and had thought that he'd seemed rather serious for her pleasure-loving sister, while at the same time realising that Nick was superficial and vain.

It had only been when their careers had brought the two of them together that she'd realised how much she was attracted to her brother-in-law.

But, unlike Tiffany and Nick, she would never have done anything about it. There was no way she would have done anything to hurt her husband or her sister, and in any case she'd known that Bryce only ever saw her as a pair of capable hands in Theatre or on the wards.

She'd been appalled to discover that Bryce had given up medicine. Why, for goodness' sake, hadn't he combined the two? she thought as she drove home later in the afternoon. Stuck to health care and flown as a hobby?

There was no need to look far for an answer. Hadn't he made it clear that he'd left the NHS because he wanted a clean break from everything that had gone before that terrible day when their respective partners had been killed and their plans exposed to those left behind?

It didn't stop Fabia from hating the waste of it, though. Doctors were always in short supply, as were nurses. At least she hadn't quit health care. She was doing what countless other women did, combining a career with motherhood. And until Bryce had appeared on the scene, she'd been reasonably content.

To have a man in her life would have been nice, she supposed, but in recent years there'd never been anyone she'd been attracted to, and having been once deceived she was wary of putting her trust in anyone again. But Bryce Hollister was a different matter. She would walk beside him blindfold if he would only give her the chance to show how much she loved him.

CHAPTER FOUR

BRYCE hadn't mentioned the cottage in Cornwall since his original suggestion and as the days went by Fabia wondered if the offer still held.

The idea of spending a fortnight in beautiful St Ives was very tempting, as was anything connected with him, and one evening she phoned him to say that she and Jessica would love to spend a couple of weeks there if the cottage was still available.

'Yes, of course it is,' he said immediately. 'I haven't said anything since I first suggested it as I thought that you felt you were being patronised. Er…you've already made it plain that you've no wish to be offered charity and I didn't want to put my foot in it further.'

Wincing at the reminder of the circumstances that had brought about the angry comment, she told him flatly 'That's in the past, Bryce. We both got carried away and you had cause to regret it.'

'And you didn't?' he questioned. 'Even though you're in love with someone else?'

'Oh, what a tangled web we weave when first we practise to deceive,' she thought, and told him, 'Yes, in spite of that. It was how you described it…a moment when we each fulfilled a need in the other.'

'And that's it?'

'Yes, that's it,' she replied steadily. 'Could we, please, get back to the reason why I rang?'

'The cottage? Yes. When do you want to go?'

'I start my leave next Saturday and, if it's all right with you, would drive down there on the Sunday. Just as long as you're sure that you don't need the place yourself.'

'I've told you, Fabia,' he insisted. 'You can have the cottage for as long as you want. I might pop down to see you during the middle weekend and we could get some beach time in with Jessica.'

'She'd love that,' she said immediately. And so would I, she thought with her spirits lifting.

'The nearest beach is Porthmeor,' he was saying, 'and no matter how often I see it the beauty of the sea and sand take my breath away. I'll bring the keys round one night this week, or maybe drop them off at the airport when I'm passing.'

'All right. Thanks, Bryce,' she said softly. 'It's very kind of you to take so much trouble over us.'

'I'm not being kind,' he said abruptly. 'I hate waste. The cottage is there doing nothing and it's a shame that it should be.'

So it wasn't especially for them that he'd offered, she thought flatly after they'd said goodbye. It was just the landlord wanting his property aired.

Well, they would do that for him. She'd felt tired of late. Some sea air was just what she needed…and maybe if Bryce did come to see them, the paradise that he'd just described might be a better place for them to draw closer than the busy confines of the airport or during his infrequent visits to her home.

What is it with you? Bryce asked himself grimly when Fabia had gone off the line. You were drawing closer to Fabia and were happy to be doing so, until she told you she loved someone else. Now you're putting up the barriers again, making it seem as if you don't care who stays at your parents' place as long as it's put to some use, when in reality it's only Fabia and Jessica you want there.

And if this guy that she's in love with is so unapproachable, why should you take a back seat? He's obviously not around so make the most of it. Whether she's in love with someone else or not, Fabia was content to be in *your* arms the other night and you've never stopped thinking about it since.

Comparing it to the love-making he'd had with Tiffany, it had been like placing wine against water. Fabia had been passionate and uninhibited, yet so tender…and what had he done? Given her the impression that he regretted letting it happen! His thought processes couldn't be functioning properly!

Yet he didn't take the keys for the cottage round to her house. With the feeling that any more private meetings wouldn't be a good idea at the moment, he called on her at the airport.

They'd just had a panic attack to deal with at the walk-in centre. A man in his mid-thirties, who was obviously very afraid of flying, had found it difficult to breathe when the boarding of his flight had been announced. He'd started with chest pains and palpitations and had generally been in a state of high anxiety.

His girlfriend had brought him to the centre to see if they could calm him down as he'd been in no fit state to make his way to the gate where the aircraft was waiting. Fabia had persuaded him to cover his nose and mouth with a small paper bag and breathe into it for a few minutes.

The symptoms had gradually decreased and, after

assuring his anxious companion that it was only a panic attack brought on by his fear of flying and not something more serious, they left to continue their journey with instructions to make the cabin crew aware of what had just happened.

It was as they were leaving that Bryce appeared, and Fabia's eyes widened when she saw that he wasn't alone. A cool-looking blonde was with him, dressed in the smart uniform of a flight purser, and he introduced her as Willow Martin.

'One of the stalwarts who try to keep life's complications at bay for me,' he said with an enigmatic smile.

With the intuition of a woman in love Fabia knew immediately that his companion was attracted to him. It was in her smile and her body language. And could she blame Willow? Bryce was free of entanglements and had a sombre sort of charisma that would appeal to most women.

Crisp dark hair above eyes blue as the sea on a summer day, set in a face that appeared hawkish until he smiled, made it inevitable that he would be noticed by the opposite sex.

Yet so deep had been his hurt from the past that no one so far had penetrated his angry disillusion until the other night when he'd taken her in his arms.

And even that joyous occasion had only brought down the barriers for a little while—they'd soon been up again. Maybe it was going to take someone like this Willow person to make a permanent break-through, Fabia thought dismally.

'So, are you all set for the holiday?' he was asking.

Fabia smiled as her thoughts veered back to basics. 'I don't know about me,' she told him, 'but Jessica is. Her bucket and spade have been in the hall ever since I spoke to you the other night.'

'That's the spirit,' he said laughingly. 'She'll have the time of her life on Porthmeor.'

As they turned to go he said casually, 'We've just got back from a long-haul flight. Willow is staying at my place overnight to save her booking in at a hotel. We're both on the Dallas flight tomorrow.'

And what would they be doing for the rest of the day...and night? Fabia wondered as they left with a last-minute comment from Bryce that he would phone the cottage on Sunday evening to make sure they'd arrived safely.

She'd nodded mutely and felt more like an encumbrance than a participant in his love life. She envied the woman who was going to spend the next few hours alone with him and was lucky enough to be working with him, too.

The cottage, like many of the dwellings of its kind in the picturesque coastal resort, was colour-washed in pale rose pink. It was clean, with basic furnishings, and it did have a lost air about it.

The first thing Fabia did on arriving was open the windows as it smelt faintly musty, and she promised herself that she would have turned what was an empty shell into a home if Bryce came down the following weekend.

But everything didn't have to hang on that. She and Jessica were there to enjoy themselves, and once they'd unpacked and eaten the snack she'd brought with her they went to explore the beach.

When she saw the stretch of smooth golden sand with the foam-tipped breakers of the Atlantic bounding up to it she caught her breath and Jessica, standing beside her in wide-eyed wonder, clapped her hands.

Bryce had been right, she thought. This place was paradise. There were surfers riding the crests of waves, dark sylph-like shapes against the sun's rays in their wetsuits. Toddlers on tiny legs crowed with delight as watchful parents took them to where the water lapped around their toes. And lovers strolled by arm in arm, bemused by the scene and each other.

She didn't dwell on them too much. It hurt when she thought about how far out of her reach Bryce was, both in distance and desire.

He rang that evening as he'd said he would, and after asking if all had been in order at the house when they'd arrived, and having been assured that it had, he said, 'And so how does Jessica like the beach?'

'She adores it,' Fabia told him, 'and so do I. If it hadn't been for us expecting your phone call, we'd still be out there.'

'So I'm to blame for dragging you away,' he said laughingly, and she joined in, thinking it would be so easy to tell him that she would leave heaven itself just to hear his voice.

'I'll ring again on Friday night before I set off,' he said, 'and should be with you in the very early morning. I've got a key so don't disturb yourself. I'll try not to make a noise and will park myself in the spare room while I catch up on some sleep.'

'Are you sure?' she questioned. 'I could make you some breakfast.'

'Yes, I'm sure. I could be with you by daybreak, which is far too early for Jessica to be disturbed.'

'All right, then,' she agreed.

It was obvious that he had no idea how she was longing to see him.

As the lazy sunfilled days passed Fabia got to know their neighbour, a laconic artist called Guy Forrester who, like many of the artistic community living in St Ives, had a small studio attached to his cottage.

He was a bearded, untidy-looking man of a similar age to herself, with a teasing smile and indisputable talent, if the many seascapes he had on view were anything to go by.

'I'd like to paint you, Fabia,' he said one day, 'with your long blonde mane blowing in the wind and the elements flattening a flimsy dress against that fantastic bone structure.'

She laughed, not thinking he was serious, but he persisted and she agreed to spend an hour each morning posing for him on the headland, while Jessica did her own thing with some paints that Guy had found for her.

'I can't pose for you tomorrow,' she told him on the Friday of the first week. My...er...friend...Bryce, who owns the cottage, is coming for the weekend, and I want to spend as much time with him as possible.'

'Ah! It's like that, is it?' he said. 'You're spoken for.'

She had to smile at the out-of-date phraseology.

'I wish I was.'

'He must be crazy, then.'

The cottage looked more homely now. The brasses had been cleaned and so had the windows. There were fresh flowers in the vases and the windows were open all the time, letting in the fresh sea breezes.

On Friday morning Fabia and Jessica shopped for the weekend's food. Fresh bread. A leg of lamb from the butchers. Crisp vegetables from the greengrocer's, along with strawberries and clotted Cornish cream for dessert.

In the evening she baked a rich fruit cake and had just taken it out of the oven when Bryce rang.

'Fabia,' he said briefly, 'I'm about to set off now. Everything all right?'

'Yes,' she told him, and before she could say anything further he was bidding her goodbye.

Bryce had been on edge all week for various reasons. Firstly, he'd had an unpleasant flight with a group of disruptive passengers who had traumatised everyone on board to such an extent that he'd asked for the police to be on hand when they landed.

And then there was Willow, who was sending out the signals that she was interested…and he didn't want to know.

But the thing that had been bugging him the most had been the thought that Fabia and Jessica hadn't been around. There had been no need to make an excuse to call at the walk-in centre to see her as she hadn't been there.

He ached to be in Cornwall with them. To feel the warm grit of the sand beneath his feet, the sea buffeting him as he plunged into its cool waters and to be back in his childhood home once more, immovable and changeless on the narrow winding street. But most of all he wanted to be with his uncomplicated sister-in-law and her child. Life had taken on a new meaning since she'd come back into his life, and everything would be wonderful if he could only put the past behind him.

Fabia heard Bryce arrive in the warm summer dawn. Heard the car stop outside and then his key in the lock. Lying rigid beneath the covers, she hugged herself with pleasure at the sounds then, reaching for a thin cotton robe, she padded down the stairs to greet him.

Bryce was depositing his belongings in the small hall when he heard Fabia's soft tread, and when he lifted his head she thought he looked tired. There was stubble on his chin and creases of weariness around his eyes.

Instead of greeting him with the delight that was washing over her, she said, 'You look as if you've had a busy week.'

He grimaced. 'You could say that. I'm certainly ready for a change of scene. I said you weren't to get up,' he remarked in a low voice with a swift glance upwards to where Jessica was sleeping. 'I've disturbed you, haven't I?'

Fabia shook her head. 'Not really. I was only catnapping. I've been listening out for you.'

Turning away, she was suddenly at a loss for words. She wanted to take him in her arms and hold him close, tell him how wonderful it was to have him with them, but she never knew how he would react. He might fall in with her mood, or put her away from him like he had that other time.

He was looking around him, his dark eyes taking in every detail of the cottage, and he was smiling.

'I haven't seen this place look so inviting since my mother was alive,' he said with his voice deepening.

'It's bright and shining, with flowers everywhere, and you fit in beautifully. You look as if you belong here.'

She wanted to tell him she belonged wherever he was, but she hadn't waited all these years to spoil it by rushing things. She'd thought ever since the night they'd given in to their feelings that it had been too soon. As spellbinding though it had been, it hadn't had the expected result. Bryce had backed off almost before she'd got her breath back, and from now on she was going to be cautious.

For one thing, she didn't know what was happening with Willow Martin, but at the first chance that came along she was going to find out. If Willow was single and without encumbrances, Bryce might see her as the ideal person if he was going to break his long fast as far as the female sex was concerned.

But there were more important things to be concerning herself with at the moment, such as feeding him after his long journey. While he went to freshen up she put bacon in the pan, poured fruit juice and brought out the clotted cream to go with cereal.

Bryce's eyes lit up when he came downstairs. 'The bacon smells divine and the rest of it is a feast for a jaded pilot. And after we've eaten I can't wait to get on the beach. I hope that the tide isn't in.'

'It is, as a matter of fact,' she told him, smiling at his enthusiasm, 'so why not catch up on some sleep first?'

'I suppose I could,' he agreed, 'and by then both things that enchant me will be there.'

As Fabia eyed him questioningly he said, 'Jessica...and the beach.'

'And where do I come into it?' she asked rashly, forgetting all her vows to be cautious in her approach.

He eyed her steadily, mouth unsmiling, eyes giving nothing away.

'You, Fabia, are the woman I've known a long time and yet never really seen until now.'

'That has a ring of truth to it,' she told him levelly. 'I'm tired of being seen as Jessica's mother or the nurse in the blue uniform who's going to sort out someone's problem. I want to be seen as a person in my own right.'

'Message received and understood,' he said with a wry smile. 'I'll consider myself told off.'

'You do that,' she advised, and went to stack the dishwasher.

Jessica was up and eager to see Uncle Bryce.

'Can't we go and wake him up?' she begged, but Fabia shook her head.

'No, Jess. He was very tired when he got here so let him sleep.'

They were in the cottage's small garden, and when Fabia looked up Guy was observing them from the gate.

'So he's arrived, has he—the fellow who owns the place?'

She nodded.

'So no posing today?' her likable neighbour was asking.

She managed a smile. 'No, not today. Like I told you, Jess and I want to spend the time with Bryce.'

He laughed.

'OK. We'll make up for it when he's gone. I wouldn't leave you for a minute if you were mine.'

Fabia was just about to tell him that she wasn't anybody's, and that they wouldn't be making up for anything, when Bryce appeared in the doorway of the cottage and his expression said that he'd overheard the conversation.

Fabia got to her feet.

'Guy is your new neighbour,' she told him. 'Jess and I have been getting to know him.'

'And Fabia has agreed to let me paint her while she's here. Her bone structure is fantastic,' Guy said as the two men shook hands.

'Really?' Bryce said coolly.

She hoped he wasn't wondering whether that same 'bone structure' was going to be painted in the nude. It appeared that he might be. When they went inside he said abruptly, 'So, what sort of a painting does Michelangelo have in mind?'

'Me standing on the headland in the wind, with my hair loose and wearing a floaty dress,' she told him, and saw his frown lighten somewhat, but she could tell that for some reason he wasn't pleased.

An excited Jessica was dancing around him, begging to go on the beach, and the moment passed, with Fabia deciding that she would be asking a few questions of her own when they were alone about a certain flight purser. And in the meantime if Bryce thought she'd become too friendly with Guy in such a short time, he was welcome to think so.

As they frolicked in and out of the water and Fabia saw how Jessica clung to Bryce, the ache was there again. Jess needed a father figure, she thought, and Bryce the fulfilment of having a child to love.

Yet there was still time for him to start a family of his own. He didn't have to settle for someone else's wife and child. Jessica was his niece. He was going to be fond of her in any case, but it didn't mean that he would want to adopt her...or marry her mother.

For all she knew, this might just be a one-off, taking time out in Cornwall with the company that was to hand and then going back to his bachelor life, which must suit him up to a point or he would have done something about it before now.

In the early afternoon Fabia went back to the cottage to put the roast in the oven, leaving Bryce and Jessica to their own devices.

The moment she appeared, Guy came out of his studio with a couple of fellow artists and she stopped to chat. She was laughing at something they'd said when one of them exclaimed, 'Look out! Here comes trouble.' When she looked up Bryce was approaching, carrying a sobbing Jessica in his arms.

'What's wrong?' she asked unbelievingly, having only just left them.

'Jessica slipped on the rocks and has cut her foot,' he said abruptly, and marched inside with her.

'Seems like you're in trouble for dawdling with the locals,' Guy said in a low voice as she hurried in after them.

It was quite a deep gash and as Fabia bathed it Bryce looked on in silence.

'Do you think it needs stitching?' she asked him as blood still oozed forth.

He took hold of the chubby little foot and examined it gently.

'Might do. Let's take her to the nearest A and E and see what they say.' With a hint of censure in his voice he added, 'I thought you came back to put the meat in the oven.'

'I did, and will do so before we set off,' she said quietly. 'I merely stopped to pass the time of day with Guy and his friends.'

'You don't have to explain to me,' he retorted. 'I just thought that you might need a reminder, that's all.'

Inside he was fuming. The pushy artist was going to be hanging around all next week after he himself had gone home and he didn't look like the kind who would hide his light under a bushel.

The fellow had wormed himself into Fabia's company by offering to paint her picture and heaven knew what he would be up to next. Bone structure indeed! He wondered just which part of Fabia's 'bone structure' he was interested in.

Yet what had it got to do with himself? She was a free agent. If she felt that she'd waited long enough for this man she was in love with to get his act together, who could blame her if she looked elsewhere? The life of the single parent could be a lonely sort of existence.

But if she was going to do that, why didn't she look in his direction? The answer to that was clear enough if he would only face up to it. He gave her no encouragement. She'd told him he carried a great big chip on his shoulder and he did, whereas she had put all that misery of long ago behind her.

The doctor in A and E decided that the cut on Jessica's foot didn't need stitching, which caused her tears to diminish.

As they'd waited to be seen Fabia had been aware of Bryce looking around him and she'd wondered if it was bringing memories back. She'd hoped so. They had a few things in common and most of them had brought bad vibes, but the time they'd spent together in health care had meant a great deal to them both. As dedicated doctor and nurse there'd always been harmony when they'd worked together. Surely he remembered that.

He'd been cuddling a tearful Jessica to him but it seemed that he might have tuned in to her thoughts when he'd said, 'It's incredible. I've been out of the hospital atmosphere for years and yet I can still feel the pull, the adrenalin building up.'

'That's because this is where you belong,' she'd said immediately. 'You were the best. Couldn't you keep flying for a leisure pursuit?'

At that moment Jessica's name had been called and in the importance of the moment the subject had been shelved.

Now it was over and they were on their way home with the little one in her mother's protective hold on the back seat of the car.

Fabia felt as if the conversation they'd had in the waiting room was hanging between them with its questions and answers, and she would dearly have liked to have brought it up again, but something told her not to.

She couldn't see Bryce ever giving up his pilot's job. He enjoyed it too much. But in her opinion job satisfaction came before pleasure and there'd been plenty of that in the old days.

The leg of lamb was crisp and tender when they got back and as Fabia prepared the rest of the meal Bryce read Jessica a story so that she would rest the injured foot.

It was a pleasant domestic scene. The man and the

child, dark heads bent over the book, and the woman preparing the meal.

Only they knew the undercurrents present and Fabia wondered what direction they would take once Jessica was tucked up in bed for the night.

It had been an eventful day, with Bryce's dawn arrival, the enchanted time they'd spent together on the beach, then the accident and the drive to hospital. Mixed in with all that had been his obvious disapproval of her acquaintance with Guy.

Surely he wasn't jealous. Yet *she* wasn't happy about the svelte, so aptly named Willow, was she? Her own relationship with Bryce was like walking through fog. One moment the mists lifted and all was clear. The next they came back down again in a solid blanket that blotted out all sense of direction. With Willow still in her mind she asked casually, 'How's your friend Willow?'

Bryce lifted his head and, pausing in his story-telling, said blandly, 'Fine. Why do you ask?'

Good question, Fabia thought wryly. Why was she asking? Because she wanted to know just how close they were.

'I wondered if she was merely an acquaintance, or if there was more to it.'

'Would I be here with Jessica and you if that were the case?' he said coolly.

'You might. This could be your good turn for the poor relations. Have you ever made love to her?' she asked quietly so that Jessica couldn't hear. 'Because if you have I hope it didn't end with a groan from the depths of your being.'

The moment the words had left her lips Fabia was

aghast. If she was hoping for a cosy evening with him she'd just put a blight on it.

There was a tight smile hovering round Bryce's mouth, and as Jessica pulled at his arm for him to continue the story he got up and went to stand in front of her.

'No, I have not slept with Willow Martin,' he said in a low voice, 'and thanks for reminding me of my inadequacies when I held you in my arms. And as we seem to be bent on clearing the air, I don't consider you to be a poor relation. To me you're rich. You have all the things that I haven't got. Generosity of spirit, peace of mind, the courage to give your love to some man who obviously doesn't deserve it. And above all you've got Jessica.'

Tears were pricking. He was the generous one. In listing her attributes he was admitting his own deficiencies. Were they ever going to be on the same wavelength?

Her belief that she'd spoilt the prospect of the evening ahead with her rash remarks was confirmed when Bryce said after they'd eaten, 'I'm going to pop out later to see an old school friend. We usually have a drink together when I come down.'

'Yes, of course,' she agreed flatly as she realised that he'd had no plans to be with her during the coming hours in any case.

Later that evening Bryce stood beside the old harbour, looking out to sea. Beached on the harbour bed was the lifeboat—a reminder that the elements weren't always kind.

It was true, what he'd told Fabia. He *was* going to

meet Ben Trewithick. They *did* always have a drink together, but it hadn't been arranged previously.

It had been a spur-of-the-moment idea because, although he and Fabia had only been together again for a few hours, the amount of soul-searching that had gone on was putting to flight all his vows to play it cool.

He knew he wouldn't be able to trust himself alone with her after the kind of day they'd had…and he knew that Ben would be in the pub. He usually was.

CHAPTER FIVE

BEN was standing at the bar, chatting to members of the fishing fraternity, of which he was one, and when he saw his friend his smile beamed across.

'Bryce!' he said. 'Good to see you. Where are you staying? I see that you've rented the cottage out.'

Bryce shook his head.

'It's not rented out. That's my sister-in-law and her little girl staying there. I'm staying with them for the weekend.'

'Your sister-in-law!' the bearded fisherman exclaimed. 'Now that you've mentioned it, I realise the blonde does look like Tiffany. But I wouldn't have thought you'd want anything to do with that family again.'

'That's the only way they are alike,' Bryce said, quickly on the defensive. 'Fabia's the exact opposite of her sister and don't forget she was hurt just as much as I was by what happened. But she's a more forgiving soul than I am.'

His friend was smiling.

'Do I detect a rare warmth in your manner?'

'No, you don't,' Bryce told him. 'We're just friends, that's all. Fabia was pregnant when Nick died and was left to bring up little Jessica on her own. We only met up again recently and I felt the least I could do was offer her the cottage if she wanted to come down here. But that's enough about me. How's life treating you?'

'Oh, I'm all right. Emma and the kids keep me in order when I'm not out on the boat. I'll drop you some fish off tomorrow if you like. How long are you here for?'

'I'll be travelling back up north in the early hours of Monday morning so, yes, the fish would be appreciated. We could have a picnic on the beach, Fabia, Jessica and myself. Bring your folks along if you like.'

Ben pulled a face.

'Can't. We're due at the mother-in-law's for high tea.'

After an hour spent chatting with Ben and the other locals Bryce was ready to go. He'd used his friend as an excuse to get away from Fabia, but now he was eager to be back.

She'd probably thought him rude, leaving her almost as soon as he'd arrived, especially as he was in St Ives for such a fleeting visit, but whenever he saw her these days he was reminded of the time they'd ended up in each other's arms.

It hadn't been long ago, yet it seemed like an eternity, and he had only himself to blame for that. After letting his guard down so completely, he'd turned the magical moment into an occasion for regret and he'd like to bet that Fabia wouldn't let anything of the kind happen again.

She deserved better than him anyway. Blowing hot and cold all the time. And in any case ever since that night she'd given no indication that she wanted anything other than friendship. For one thing, there was still the mystery man in the background, obviously needing a prod in the right direction. Exactly how long had she known him? he wondered. He must have come on the scene after Nick died, but where was he now, and just how out of reach was he?

His step quickened. Any man who kept Fabia dangling was a fool. With regard to himself, he was in a prime position to get to know her all over again and yet wasn't doing all that much about it, even though the very sight of her made him weak with protective tenderness.

When he went inside Bryce was immediately reminded that there was someone else bent on getting close to her. He could hear voices, and as the door of the sitting room swung open his face tightened. That artist was lounging beside her on the sofa with one arm draped around her shoulders, and Bryce was amazed how annoyed he was to find him there.

Fabia smiled when she saw him and got to her feet, but he had no answering beam for her. It was none of his business who she chose to spend her time with, and he'd made sure she couldn't spend the evening with him by rushing off to the pub, but it wasn't stopping him from observing them coldly.

'I was just about to make supper,' she told him.

Bryce shook his head and pointed upwards in the direction of the spare room.

'None for me, thanks. I'm going to have an early night.'

The other man was uncoiling himself off the sofa.

''Fraid it's the same for me, too, Fabia. Not the early night, but some friends are coming round.'

When they'd both disappeared, Fabia went to the window and stood looking out over the headland. If it had been anyone else but Bryce glowering at her she would have thought he was jealous, but that was hardly likely.

Or had he looked like that because he thought she was leading Guy on and it had reminded him of Tiffany's flirtatious ways? He had some cheek if that was the case. She was free to be with whom she chose and Guy had only popped in for a second to see when she would be able to sit for him again.

She'd been disappointed when Bryce had taken himself off to the pub, but had told herself that she didn't own the man and probably never would. There was nothing in his manner to indicate that he'd come to Cornwall especially to be with Jessica and her. He probably saw himself in the role of responsible land-lord and had merely come to check that all was well.

The main thing was that he was here…with them…under the same roof, and it had been his idea that he join them. For once fate was being kind. There was still tomorrow. Maybe they could make up for lost time then.

A sound from behind had her turning swiftly and he was there in the doorway, observing her unsmil-ingly as he said, 'I forgot to mention that Ben is going to bring some fish round tomorrow. How do you fancy us having a picnic on the beach? We can either cook it first or take the barbecue up on the headland.'

'So you're not annoyed with me?' she said slowly.

He didn't meet her gaze.

'No, of course not. Why?'

'You seemed to be in a hurry to get to the pub earlier and didn't seem pleased to see Guy here when you got back.'

'It's none of my business who you want to flirt with,' he said in a softer tone, which was annoying rather than reassuring. 'And if I seemed in a rush earlier, it was because I hadn't seen Ben for ages.'

Bryce was squirming inwardly. What was the matter with him? He was being officious and untruthful almost in the same breath. The peace of mind that he'd striven for had been disappearing fast since meeting Fabia again. She was serene and uncomplicated and he was disgruntled and suspicious. Therein lay the difference.

But the serenity that he was crediting her with had been ruffled by his comment about flirting, and there was anger sparking in the violet eyes challenging his.

'Guy Forrester is just a friendly acquaintance,' she said coolly, 'and if he's coming on to me, it's not of my doing. I've told you once, Bryce, that I'm in love with someone else and that isn't going to change.'

'Yet you were attracted to me that night.'

'Yes. I was, wasn't I? Which, I suppose, made you think that flirting is the norm in my family.'

Is he blind? she thought dismally. And am I a coward? Why don't I tell him the truth? The answer was there almost before she'd asked herself the question. She was Tiffany's sister, and she knew that would always be a barrier to him.

'I don't remember making any such comment.'

'Of course not, but it wouldn't stop you thinking it.'

He sighed.

'Don't let's spend the weekend sniping at each other, Fabia. I know that I started it and I'm sorry. Maybe it would have been better if I hadn't come.'

She smiled and with her tranquillity restored protested, 'Don't say that, Bryce. Jessica loves having you around.'

'And you?'

'Yes…me, too. We're both short of male company.'

'That's all right, then,' he said equably, aware that
she could have been more enthusiastic.

As silence fell between them Fabia knew that she
didn't want him to keep to his intention of having an
early night. He'd already come back downstairs once
and she wanted him to stay down…with her.

'Why don't we sit in the garden for a while?' she
suggested casually.

'Yes, why not?' he agreed. 'It's too nice a night to
be wasted. I love this place. It was paradise to grow
up in.'

'But not now a suitable base for a busy pilot?'

As they seated themselves on the bench in the cottage's small garden he smiled wryly.

'Hardly. After my initial training in Spain I moved
around a lot. Why I returned to the area where I'd
lived with Tiffany I don't know. Maybe it was to lay
her ghost. The last thing I ever expected was to find
you working at the airport.'

'You wouldn't have sought me out otherwise,
would you?' she questioned with unconscious wist-
fulness. 'Not having given me a thought during all
that time.'

'I did think of you,' he admitted, 'but usually in
relation to Tiffany. Now I'm really getting to know
you I see how mistaken I was to cut you out of my
life.'

'But we worked together. Surely you had my mea-
sure from that. We were colleagues. I wasn't just your
wife's sister.'

'Yes, I know, but our work at the hospital was in
a separate compartment in my life.' He couldn't bring

himself to tell her that it had only been since meeting her again he'd realised how much her presence had meant to him in those days.

'So it would seem' she said drily.

'I imagine it was the same for you,' he said.

Fabia didn't answer. She could hardly tell him that for her the time they'd worked in Theatre and on the wards had been one of the happiest periods of her life. Not now that he'd made it crystal clear just how little it had mattered to him.

'Don't you ever miss being in medicine?' she asked.

'Of course I do. When we took Jessica to hospital I could feel the pull. Just as I have at other times when I've been in those sorts of surroundings.'

'Those first months after I quit were hard to cope with, but I was besieged with a desperate desire to put everything connected with that part of my life behind me. As I told you once before, I'd always wanted to fly. I feel free of all encumbrances when I'm up there in the sky.'

There wasn't a lot Fabia could say to that and as silence descended once more the magic of the night took over. The tide was coming in. She could hear its rhythmic thudding against the beach as each breaker came surging in.

On the horizon a summer sun was setting like a fiery golden ball. Gulls diving and swirling around the headland screeched in the distance and the smell of flowers drifted on the night air.

It was a night for lovers, she thought, warm and sultry. Soon the velvet darkness would descend and what would they do? Each go to their rooms beneath the whitewashed eaves, to lie restless and unsated?

That was how she would be, and she felt that in spite of his hands-off attitude Bryce would feel the same.

She got to her feet and he said immediately, 'Where are you going?'

'To check on Jess,' she told him. 'Just to make sure she's all right. I'm hoping that she's not had too much sun.'

He sank back against the wooden bench and looked up at her with a questioning bright blue gaze.

'Why don't I open a bottle of wine for when you come back down?'

'Why not, indeed?' she agreed. Anything to keep him with her for a little while longer.

It was dark by the time Bryce had filled their glasses, and as they toasted each other Fabia could feel the chemistry between them reaching out like a magnet.

Bryce hadn't touched her, but the look in his eyes was a caress. It was going to be like that other night, she thought breathlessly, their need of each other blotting out all reason. If it happened again, surely he would realise they belonged together?

The sound of voices on the night air broke the spell and to her dismay Guy and his friends appeared, damp and glistening from a late swim.

They perched on the garden wall, laughing and chatting, and there was no way Fabia could ask them to go. She couldn't tell them they'd just interrupted an enchanted moment and she knew that Bryce wasn't going to send them away. After all, they were her acquaintances.

He was smiling but there was a grimness about it that told her having to suffer the company of the bearded artist twice in one night was once too much for him.

'I'm turning in, Fabia,' he said levelly. 'See you in the morning.' She knew that this time he really meant it.

When the others had gone she stayed there in the garden, loth to go up to her solitary bed. Maybe it was for the best that they'd been interrupted, she told herself. In spite of the attraction between them, Bryce had to be sure that a commitment to her was something he was able to enter into without the trappings of the past bugging him. And something told her that he hadn't yet come that far.

After a restless night Fabia awoke to the sound of voices down below. She could hear Jessica's high notes mingling with Bryce's deeper tones and she lay back against the pillows, savouring the moment.

When she went downstairs he was giving Jessica her breakfast. Her small daughter waved a milky spoon in her direction and said, 'Uncle Bryce said I mustn't wake you up, Mummy.'

Fabia smiled across to where he was buttering toast at the kitchen table. 'That was very thoughtful of him.'

Her spirits were lifting by the moment. The everyday domestic scene put everything from the night before into perspective. Bryce was here because he wanted to be. That was clear from the way he was observing them. So why didn't she just accept that and put on hold any other yearnings she might have?

The day stretched ahead of them and when he left in the early hours of Monday morning to go back to his flying duties she would console herself with the thought that at least they'd spent the weekend together.

That kind of reasoning lasted until the moment Bryce was ready to leave and then the longing to feel his arms around her became so acute she felt weak with the intensity of it.

But he was putting his case in the boot and slinging his jacket onto the back seat as if regret at parting was the last thing on his mind.

A vision of Willow came to Fabia's mind, sleek and elegant in the smart uniform of the cabin crew. She thought that he would be continually surrounded by her and others like her and one day he might find in their midst a woman far more acceptable than an ex-sister-in-law with a child. Bryce surely wasn't intending keeping to his celibate state for ever.

He looked up and saw her expression. Eyeing her questioningly, he asked, 'Why so serious? I'm not flying to the moon tomorrow. Just the Dallas run.'

'I was thinking about Willow Martin.'

Dark brows were rising above surprised blue eyes.

'Willow? What has she got to do with anything?'

'She's very attractive.'

His face had tightened.

'For goodness' sake, Fabia! So are a thousand other women, but it doesn't mean that I'm going to do anything about it. Willow's been married twice and divorced the same number of times. I'm not into that sort of territory.'

She was already wishing she'd kept her mouth shut, but her hasty comment had done one thing. If Bryce wasn't falling over himself to make moves on her, at least it seemed he wasn't interested in anyone else.

He reached out and touched her cheek briefly. 'Enjoy the rest of your stay, Fabia. I'll be in touch once you're back. I've left a little something for Jessica for when she wakes up in the morning. Take care of her.'

She smiled. They were on familiar ground now.

'I always do,' she told him, and off he went.

As the car ate up the miles through the southern counties Bryce was thinking about those moments outside the cottage before he'd left.

He wondered if Fabia ever looked in the mirror and, if she did, what she saw. She'd stood beside him, the breeze from the ocean lifting the long golden strands of her hair and flattening the soft cotton top she'd been wearing against the firm mounds of her breasts. And as she'd quizzed him as to where his heart lay it had taken all his strength of will not to take her in his arms and answer her question with actions rather than words.

If his heart was in anyone's keeping, it was hers. But she didn't seem to see that as likely and he supposed he couldn't blame her. He kept giving out different kinds of signals and she couldn't help but be aware of it.

He'd often thought that one day his wariness would diminish and he would fall in love again. But he'd been in no hurry and never in a thousand years had he visualised it being his wife's sister who would be the one to make him come alive again.

That was the catastrophic part of it. With any other woman in his arms and his bed, the memories of Tiffany would have faded, but Fabia was a constant reminder of what had gone on in the past. Meeting her again had brought it all back again just as he was settling into a sort of numb contentment, and there was a grim irony about it.

He wasn't usually a ditherer. He took life by the horns and got to grips with it. He'd faced up to his wife's deceit all those years ago with a sort of grim stoicism, and if he hadn't been able to let go of the hurt it had caused, no one knew it but himself.

When he'd met Fabia again he'd been completely thrown, and at the time had had no intention of pursuing the relationship, but he'd reckoned without her generosity of spirit, her physical attractions...and the captivating Jessica. And now he was trapped in a situation where common sense said, Walk away or you'll bring hurt to yourself and them.

When he'd gone Fabia had found an oblong-shaped box, gift-wrapped, on the table at the side of Jessica's bed, and realised that he must have brought it with him as they hadn't done any shopping while he'd been there.

The sight of it brought the lump to her throat that always came when she thought about Bryce having no children of his own. He was gentle and protective with her daughter and she sensed that it wasn't just because she was his niece. It went deeper than that. Being with Jessica fulfilled a need in him and in return Bryce filled the gap in her life that Nick had left.

When she awakened to find a doll inside the package with rosy cheeks, long eyelashes, pouting lips and inside it the mechanisms to perform various bodily functions, the little girl crowed with delight and said, 'I wish that Uncle Bryce could be my daddy.'

Fabia turned away with no ready answer for her. Jessica was too young to realise the improbability of that ever happening.

The days of their second week in Cornwall flew, with Fabia and Jessica spending lazy days on the beach and Guy working on the painting whenever the opportunity arose.

He was still very friendly but Fabia knew that Bryce's visit at the weekend had made him back off. For that she was grateful as, apart from a genuine liking for the bearded artist, she had no real interest in him and her feelings for Bryce were making her life complicated enough without any other side issues.

When the phone rang on their last night at the cottage she answered it eagerly, knowing that there was only one person who would be calling, and when Bryce's voice came over the line her world righted itself.

Fabia had enjoyed the past week but there'd been something missing and she hadn't had to look far to know what it was. After having him with them over the previous weekend the days that had followed had lacked purpose. She was more than ready to get back to her home surroundings and the airport where she would know he was somewhere nearby if she didn't get to see him.

'So how's it gone?' he was asking.

'Lovely,' she breathed, referring more to the sound of his voice than the second week of the holiday. 'How has it been with you?'

'Oh, so-so. Long flights followed by long sleeps Nothing very exciting, I'm afraid. What time are you leaving?'

'Early in the morning. Before the northbound traffic builds up.'

'Good thinking. Drive carefully, Fabia. Has Jessica enjoyed herself?'

'Yes. She loved the doll and has played with it constantly. It was kind of you to think of her,' she told him.

'And that artist?'

'Guy? Oh, he's been around occasionally, finishing off the painting and generally being neighbourly. He reckons he'll miss us when we're gone, but that's Guy just being Guy.

'Where are you scheduled for next week?' she went on, anxious to keep him on the line. 'Anywhere exciting?'

'New York and the Dallas run again,' he said casually, 'and then I have a few days' leave coming up.'

'Jessica's missing you,' she said softly, 'even though she's loth to leave the sea and the sand.'

'Is she?' he said slowly, and she wondered if he was going to ask if she was, too. But he didn't give her the opportunity to say her piece, just told her to drive carefully once more and left it at that.

As she was replacing the receiver the doorbell rang, and when she opened the door Guy was on the step, holding the finished painting.

It was good, she thought as she stood back to look at it...very good.

He held it out to her and said, 'Here, take it.'

She beamed her thanks and wondered why she couldn't be attracted to someone like him, easygoing, uncomplicated, no past to make him miserable as far as she knew.

But life wasn't like that, was it? she told herself after he'd gone. She'd loved Bryce Hollister for a long time. It came as naturally to her as breathing and nothing was going to change that.

She'd wondered sometimes what it had been about her flighty sister that had so ensnared him. But knowing the man for what he was, Fabia knew that when he made a commitment he stuck to it. That was why the hurt had gone so deep.

And what of herself? Why had she found it so easy to forgive? Had it been because she'd found life with Nick less than fulfilling?

If he ever found out that she loved him, would Bryce see that as a form of adultery, even though she would never have done anything about it while their two partners had been alive? After the accident the opportunity had been denied her because before she'd been able to gather her wits Bryce had sold up and gone to heaven knew where.

When Fabia and Jessica got home, Maggie greeted her with the news that her pilot friend had beaten her to it and had stocked up the fridge and brought fresh bread and milk for their return.

'He had to tell me what he was up to,' the flame-haired mother of two told her, 'as he needed the key to take the stuff inside. What a package you've got there, Fabia,' she teased. 'Caring and dishy with it. You want to hang onto him.'

Fabia smiled. Maggie made it sound so simple. But she was right in one respect—it was a caring thing that Bryce had done and, instead of always having to fend for herself, it was nice to have someone do something for her for once.

When she rang to thank him Willow answered the phone and her spirits sank. Was the elegant purser staying with Bryce during another stopover? Why didn't she get a place of her own? she thought irritably, and it must have come through in her voice as when Bryce came on the line he said immediately, 'What's wrong? You sound as if someone has ruffled your feathers.'

'No, nothing like that,' she assured him hastily, remembering why she wanted to speak to him. 'I'm just ringing to thank you for shopping for us. It was very kind of you and much appreciated as I was tired when we got back.'

'My pleasure,' he said smoothly. 'Is Jessica all right after the journey?'

'Mmm, she's fine. At the moment she's renewing her acquaintance with the boys next door as if she's been away for ever.'

He laughed.

'It probably seems like that to a five-year-old.'

'Willow answered the phone,' she said after a moment's silence. 'I take it that she's staying over.'

'Yes,' he said smoothly. 'We've got a long-haul flight tomorrow and will be turning in shortly.'

'In that case, I won't keep you,' she said flatly, with a vision of them 'turning in' in the same bed, even though he had told her he wasn't interested in anyone else.

Couldn't Bryce see that she was asking for reassurance? she thought when they'd finished speaking. That she needed to know that he cared?

But did he? He was solicitous about their well-being, but that could be from a delayed sense of responsibility, making up for all the years when she'd been so alone. There was nothing to indicate that it went any further as every time the chemistry between them started to work he backed off.

It was incredible to think they'd once melted with the passion and tenderness of two people meant for each other. Now it was as if she'd dreamt it.

It was chaotic at the walk-in centre on Fabia's first day back at the airport. School holidays always brought more emergency health problems, and today was no exception.

A toddler had fallen off one of the seats in the departure lounge and knocked himself out, and his anxious parents had brought him to be treated.

Giles had insisted on sending for an ambulance, even though the child was beginning to come round, which left the parents relieved and frantic at the same time. A delay had been announced on their flight but there was nothing to say that they would be in time to catch it under the circumstances.

'Any period of unconsciousness is worrying,' Fabia told them when they remonstrated about taking him to hospital. 'See how your child's head is swelling and he's disorientated. It's surprising really as the floor is carpeted.'

'He hit the side of a luggage trolley,' the father said. 'His mother should have been watching him better.'

'Oh, so it's my fault, is it?' she cried.

Fabia was examining the boy's eyes to see if he was focusing properly, and when it appeared that he was she told them, 'See what the paramedics say when they get here. It's up to them if they take him to A and E. If he doesn't go, you'll need to keep a close watch on him during the flight and afterwards.'

By the time the ambulance arrived he was sitting up and gazing around him blearily, a large swelling on the side of his head.

'There could be inward bleeding,' she told the paramedics. 'It feels soft and squelchy beneath the skin.'

They agreed and, with the frustrated parents having to accept that their son's well-being was more important than catching a plane, they stretchered him to the ambulance.

On their heels came a teenage girl, Ibiza bound, with a gastric upset. She'd been vomiting ever since arriving at the airport and her friends had brought her to the centre to see if they could do anything to stop the sickness.

There were no other symptoms than the nausea, and it was difficult to tell if it was nerves, a bug, or something she'd eaten. The only thing was to advise no food but plenty of liquids and hope that the sickness passed before she boarded her flight.

An elderly woman had fallen coming down the steps of the coach that had brought her to the airport, and antiseptic ointment and a bandage had been put on a badly grazed shinbone.

She was followed by a child who had pushed a bead down his ear. Fortunately it hadn't gone too far in, and with a pair of tweezers Fabia managed to get a grip on the bead and remove it.

They'd all been reasonably minor problems, except to those experiencing them, and it continued like that for most of the morning until midday when a far more serious health problem arose.

CHAPTER SIX

THE mother of a family had been taken ill shortly after arriving on a flight from Africa and her bewildered husband, with three tearful children in tow, had brought her to the walk-in centre.

Within seconds the usual orderly atmosphere had become pandemonium. There was a language problem and the husband was shouting and gesticulating, trying to make himself understood, while the children howled in the background.

The woman, on the point of collapse, was holding her head and groaning loudly, and before Fabia and the other nurse on duty could help her into one of the consulting rooms she sank down onto the carpet in Reception with a loud wailing cry.

It was Giles's day off so there was no senior medic to consult, and as her colleague picked up the phone to summon an ambulance Fabia knelt beside the writhing figure of the woman.

She appeared to be suffering from severe head pains and was trying to protect her eyes from the light. Beneath the loose brightly coloured garment she was wearing it was clear to see that her stomach was distended.

Her pulse was racing, her skin burning to the touch. She could barely keep her head up and was obviously in agony. As Fabia began to loosen her clothes she vomited. While the other nurse cleaned her up, Fabia was checking the woman's heartbeat when a voice

Play The Lucky Hearts Game

and get...
FREE BOOKS & a FREE GIFT...
YOURS to KEEP!

Yes! I have scratched off the silver card. Please send me my **FREE BOOKS** and **FREE MYSTERY GIFT**. I understand that I am under no obligation to purchase any books as explained on the back of this card. I am over 18 years of age.

Scratch Here! then look below to see what you can claim...

M3JI

Mrs/Miss/Ms/Mr _____ Initials _____

BLOCK CAPITALS PLEASE

Surname _____

Address _____

_____

Postcode _____

Twenty-one gets you
4 FREE BOOKS and a
MYSTERY GIFT!

Twenty gets you
1 FREE BOOK and a
MYSTERY GIFT!

Nineteen gets you
1 FREE BOOK!

TRY AGAIN!

THE READER SERVICE™
FREE BOOK OFFER
FREEPOST CN81
CROYDON
CR9 3WZ

NO STAMP
NECESSARY
IF POSTED IN
THE U.K. OR N.I.

said from behind, 'It could be some sort of tropical disease. Let me see her chest.'

She swung round from her kneeling position and observed the owner of those calm tones with relief. She'd been longing to see Bryce again, and there he was, placing his overnight case on a nearby seat and preparing to kneel beside her.

There was a red rash on the woman's chest, and Bryce nodded as if he wasn't surprised.

'I could be wrong, but I've seen this kind of thing before. It could actually be meningitis. But only a spinal tap will be able to confirm whether I'm right.'

'It will be a notifiable illness if it is, then,' she said anxiously, with a quick glance at the woman's family who had now subsided into silence.

He nodded.

'Yes. It can be contagious via throat and respiratory secretions but if it's bacterial it is usually treatable by antibiotics as long as the fever isn't too entrenched.'

The doors swung open at that moment, announcing the speedy arrival of the emergency services, and as paramedics took over it was left to the staff of the centre to try to explain to the woman's husband where she was being taken and that some sort of transport would be arranged for them to follow her.

When order was eventually restored Fabia said, 'How could she be so ill and no one be aware of it on the flight?'

'Meningitis strikes suddenly, sometimes in a matter of hours. Fever, headache and stiff neck are usually the first symptoms and wouldn't necessarily tell the sufferer that something so serious was wrong. They may not have appeared until after she boarded the flight. I remember a couple of cases from when we were on the wards. Maybe you weren't around at the time.'

Fabia smiled, the pleasure of being with him once again lifting her spirits.

'How are you?' he asked. 'Glad to be back on the job?'

'Yes,' she told him, looking him straight in the eye. 'And the reason for that is standing right beside me.'

She watched his face close up and thought that nothing had changed since he'd left Cornwall. As if to prove her right, he said blandly, 'You mean my turning up just at the right moment?'

'Yes, if that's how you want to see it,' she said coolly, and with irritation rising in her went on to comment, 'Although I am trained to deal with this sort of emergency. It's all part of the job.'

'Well, of course,' he countered smoothly. 'I never meant to infer that it wasn't and I could be wrong in my diagnosis.'

'But you don't think you are.'

She couldn't resist the sarcasm, still ruffled that he hadn't picked up on what she'd said. But if Bryce chose to ignore it when she was giving out a signal there wasn't a lot she could do, except tell him the bald truth—and she might be driven to do that one of these days.

'We'll have to wait and see, won't we?' he was remarking in the same smooth manner. 'It would be better if I was wrong as you've been in contact with the woman's body fluids. Myself less so and *I've* had all the vaccinations with flying to so many different countries.'

Fabia shuddered. The thought of what would happen if ever she was ill was always there. What would

Jessica do without her? Maggie was good and would offer to have her, but she had a family of her own to look after. If Jess had to be taken into care, it would be dreadful.

'What's the matter?' Bryce was asking. 'It will be time to worry if the tests are positive.'

'Yes,' she agreed, 'but let's hope that it doesn't come to that,' and on a lighter note she added, 'Might I ask what brought you here? Are you flying out or in?'

'In, of course, or I wouldn't have been able to assist. Where's your boss, by the way? Shouldn't you report back to him?'

'It's Giles's day off. But he'll see it in the report book when he comes in tomorrow. If the hospital is going to have to grow a culture, it might be a few days before any results are through…and you didn't answer my question.'

'I'm here because I wanted to see you.'

'Why?'

'Does there have to be a reason?'

'Yes.'

'All right, then, I stopped by because I hope that we're friends and that's what friends do…check on each other's well-being.' It was a muted description of his feelings. They went much deeper than that.

'I see.'

'Yes. I'm sure you do,' he said crisply. He turned to leave. 'I'd like to pop round to see Jessica if that's all right with you. I've missed her.'

Fabia swallowed hard. No mention of missing her. Just her small daughter. Yet shouldn't she be thankful for that? Love came in many guises and the love of an adult for a child was just as precious as that of a man for a woman, or a woman for a man.

'Yes, of course,' she told him with more warmth in her voice. 'You're welcome any time.'

'This evening, then? Before she goes to bed?'

'Mmm. Why not?' There was amusement in the violet eyes meeting his. 'Jess will be able to show you all the things that her new doll can do. Be prepared.'

He'd done it again, Bryce thought wryly as he let himself into his own quiet abode a little later. Put up the defences. Given Fabia the impression that he was only seeking her company to see her daughter. But if she was in love with some other guy, what was the point of letting her see how she was affecting him?

As she'd stood before him in her neat blue uniform, with the aura of the sea winds and the Cornish sun still upon her, she'd never been more desirable.

The resemblance to Tiffany still threw him every time he saw her, but there were many differences and the more he observed Fabia, the more he realised that she wasn't a clone of his dead wife. She was her own sweet self and why he couldn't accept that instead of hedging every time he saw her he didn't know.

He'd never cheated on anyone in his life and when he'd found that his wife and brother-in-law hadn't played to the same rules a black cloud of mistrust of life in general had engulfed him. But of late he'd felt that he'd let it submerge him for long enough.

As his thoughts veered away to the episode at the walk-in centre he decided that when he saw Fabia tonight he would insist that she follow up the case of the woman with the suspected meningitis. If the results of the tests were positive, then she would need to be on the alert for any symptoms of the illness.

And in the meantime he was going to banish everything else from his mind except the thought of some more quality time with his small niece and her mother.

Jessica was waiting for Bryce with her nose pressed against the window as he pulled up outside the cottage, and when Fabia opened the door to him the little girl flew into his arms.

As their eyes met above Jessica's brown curls, Fabia saw the hunger in his, and the familiar lump came into her throat. She would give him children, she thought wistfully, if he would let her. She had enough love for both of them and longed to fill the aching void that the past had left in him.

But bringing about that state of affairs was another matter. She hadn't forgotten their meeting earlier and his deliberate misunderstanding of what she'd meant when she'd told him that he was the reason she was glad to be back.

Their relationship seemed all the time to be moving forward a little and then sliding back a lot. Hardly a recipe for peace of mind and contentment.

But at least Bryce was here…with them…and it was at his request. He hadn't needed persuading. He'd wanted to come and, as Jessica climbed up on to his knee and began to show him the workings of the doll, Fabia thought that here was something she could give him without any strings attached—the love of her fatherless child.

When Jessica was asleep a silence fell between them, as if the bond that had been there before had been broken with her departure. He's going to go now, she thought, and if he does I will know for sure that I don't count.

But surprisingly Bryce was settling down as if he was in no rush to depart and there was an air of purpose about him. Her heartbeat quickened. He had something important to say, she could feel it. When he cleared his throat she found she was holding her breath.

'Fabia,' he said solemnly.

'Yes?' she breathed.

'I want you to follow up the African woman's treatment—find out the result of the tests. If it's what I think it might be, don't delay if you develop any symptoms.'

She slumped back against the cushions of the chair. So much for anything other than the mundane. When she didn't answer he said, 'Did you hear me?'

'Yes, I heard you,' she told him flatly. 'Though why you should think I need to be told to do that I don't know. I have been in health care for a long time. I do know about the risks we take. If there's any cause for alarm, I'll go straight to the hospital.'

She was being ungracious and knew it. She ought to be grateful for his concern but she wanted more than that. She wanted to be loved, not fussed over.

Bryce was looking at her with raised brows.

'What is it with you today, Fabia? You're edgy. Don't you want me to be concerned about you? Someone has to be. This man that you're hankering after doesn't deserve you. Where is he? Who is he? How long have you known him? Before Nick died or after?'

The questions were coming thick and fast. He

hadn't asked them before but now, suddenly, it was imperative to know. But when the answer came he wished he'd never brought the matter up.

'I've known him a long time…since before Nick died.'

'So you were having an affair, too?'

The question cut through the air like a knife.

'No.'

'No? So you've never slept with him?'

'No.'

'But you *were* in love with someone else while you were married to Nick. I thought you were different, Fabia,' he said slowly, 'but it would seem that I was the only one of the four of us who wasn't unfaithful.'

Tell him! the voice of reason was saying. Don't let Bryce think badly of you, even if it does end in humiliation. He's got it all wrong and only you can put it right.

But pride was overcoming reason. How dared he judge her? It was clear that it was still there, the tendency to class her with Tiffany. She would like to see his face were she to explain that he was the one she was 'hankering' after, that he was the one she'd fallen in love with all that time ago.

'Fine,' she said smoothly, 'if that's what you want to think. Though I have to say that you're very quick to pass judgement.'

'Maybe, but when the facts are placed before me, what is there to say?'

'How about, "It doesn't matter to me what happened in the past, Fabia. I like you for the person you are"?' she rapped back.

Bryce was on his feet. Looking down at her, he said, 'I'm sorry you don't like me fussing over you.

I'll remember that in future. And as for the rest of it, I hope that the wet lettuce that you are in love with will come up to scratch one day so that Jessica will have a father.' And before she could tell him that he was the only father she wanted for her daughter, he had gone, striding out into the summer night.

When he'd gone she stayed there, unmoving. Tonight's charade was just one more proof that they weren't going anywhere. She'd been longing for him to tell her that he loved her, but the only thing on his mind had been the risk of her catching meningitis, and in her pique she'd let him jump to all the wrong conclusions. They were further apart than ever now.

In the week that followed there was no further contact between them. Fabia picked up the phone to ring Bryce several times but replaced it before making the call. Common sense told her to leave things as they were, though she did have a good excuse for getting in touch.

The African woman had been diagnosed as having bacterial meningitis and was being treated in the hospital's isolation unit. Bryce had been right and once again she was aware of the waste of his medical expertise. Working with him had always been a joy... and loving him a cross to bear.

Eventually she did ring him, having decided that it was only common courtesy to inform him of the outcome of the incident they'd been involved in at the centre.

As she waited for him to answer there was tension in her. They hadn't parted on the best of terms. Would he want to talk to her? When his voice came over the line he sounded pleasant enough, though somewhat guarded, and, anxious to pass on the message without personalities creeping in, Fabia launched into the details regarding the sick woman.

'I see,' he said slowly when she'd finished. 'Are you feeling OK?'

'Yes,' she told him. When nothing else seemed to be forthcoming, she forgot about her intention to be brief and asked, 'Is that all you've got to say?'

'What do you expect?' he questioned coolly. 'I'm not allowed to warn you about the dangers of catching the disease, and if I'd said I wasn't surprised to hear the diagnosis you'd have thought I was basking in my own conceit. So it seems that least said, soonest mended.'

'At which you are an expert,' she flashed back angrily. And before he could ask what she'd meant by that she replaced the receiver.

It was in the middle of the following week that Fabia began to feel ill with stomach cramps, a severe headache, and a temperature.

Fear had her in its grip the moment the symptoms began to appear, and underlying it there was shame for the way she'd been so flip with regard to Bryce's warning.

As she prepared to go to Outpatients, bypassing her GP's surgery, which would be full of people who already had something wrong with them without having to come into contact with a possible meningitis sufferer, Fabia knew she had to take Jessica with her. Maggie wouldn't want her children put at risk because her next-door neighbour had been in contact with a serious disease.

But what would happen to her daughter if she was

admitted and placed in isolation until the appropriate tests had been carried out? she thought anxiously.

She'd rung Giles at the centre and put him in the picture, and now she was waiting to be seen with a fixed smile on her face for her daughter and dread clutching at her heart.

It was one of the loneliest moments of her life. With any other health problem she would have been able to turn to Maggie, but not with this.

A nurse was approaching with a smiling hospital social worker by her side. 'The doctor will see you now, Mrs Ferguson,' she said, 'and Angela will sit with your little girl while you're being attended to.'

As Fabia dragged herself to her feet she thought that this was the worst moment of her life.

'You do have some of the symptoms of meningitis,' the doctor in A and E said when he'd examined her, 'but not all of them, yet. I'm going to admit you and we'll do a spinal tap so that we can test your spinal fluid as that is the only way to be sure if you do have the illness or not.'

Fabia nodded. In a grim practical way it made sense, but the thought of being separated from Jessica was unbearable. She was a well-adjusted, secure little thing, but they'd never been apart before. How would she cope with strangers?

When she opened the door of the consulting room to go and wait for someone to escort her to the wards, she could hear Jessica laughing and her anguish deepened as she thought how soon tears would follow.

But it wasn't the social worker who was entertaining her daughter. Bryce was sitting beside her and the moment he saw her he was on his feet, holding tightly to Jessica's hand as they approached her. In that moment it was as if the sun had come from behind cloud.

'What's the verdict?' he asked briefly as tears pricked her eyes.

'As to be expected,' she croaked. 'A spinal tap then a culture to confirm if I've got the bacteria and then, if I have, I'll be treated in the isolation ward with antibiotics. How did you know where we were?'

'I rang the centre to speak to you and Giles told me what was going on.'

She sank down onto the nearest chair.

'I'm afraid for Jessica,' she told him wretchedly. 'Something like this happening has always been at the back of my mind. What am I going to do, Bryce? This is what comes of having no partner or family to turn to.'

'You've got me,' he said. 'I'll look after her. I'm already on a couple of weeks' leave. I'll extend it if need be. If it's all right with you, I'll move into your place, as I think she'll be better in familiar surroundings.'

Relief was washing over her in a gladsome tide.

'You would do this for me,' she whispered.

His voice was gentle. 'I've just said I would, haven't I? We don't want Jessica's happy little world to come crashing down, do we?'

If she hadn't been so overcome it might have occurred to her that Bryce was putting Jessica first again, but even if it had, she was so grateful that she would have forgiven him.

'Mrs Ferguson, they're ready for you on the ward,' the nurse was saying. 'Do you want your husband to bring you some things when he comes to visit?'

She shook her head, ignoring the nurse's mistake.

'I brought the necessities with me as I was expecting to be admitted. Don't visit me, Bryce, until we're sure what I've got. I know you would be gowned and would scrub up afterwards, but I can't bear the thought of Jess picking up meningitis.

'We can speak on the phone. I won't be completely out of touch.' Her voice softened. 'And thanks from the bottom of my heart for being there for us.'

'It's the least I can do, Fabia,' he said sombrely, and as the nurse picked up Fabia's case he said to Jessica, 'Wave bye-bye to Mummy.' Thinking that it was all some part of a game now that he was there, she did as she was told.

The culture had been set up, the first dose of antibiotics administered, in case she did have the infection, and in the quietness of a small side ward Fabia lay back against the pillows in groggy thankfulness.

Her head and neck ached, the gastric problems were still there, but her mind was at peace. If there was one person she could trust to care for Jessica, it was Bryce. Whatever reservations he might have about herself he loved Jessica and it was typical of the man that he would offer to look after her.

His integrity was second to none. Maybe that was why he found it so hard to cope with the failings of others, she thought wryly. Yet he wasn't intolerant. She'd seen patience and understanding in his dealings with the sick and nervous newcomers to health care.

To be loved by such a man would be heaven on earth, but in the meantime she had to content herself with the thought that at least one of them had triumphed. Her daughter had found a place in his heart.

*   *   *

They rang in the early evening. Bryce came on the line first, wanting to know what was being done regarding her condition and asking how she was feeling.

'Still pretty rough,' she told him, 'but you've given me peace of mind, and I can't thank you enough for that, Bryce.'

'There is no need for you to keep thanking me,' he told her. 'I'm the lucky one in all this. You're sick and Jessica's without her mum. And much as I'm going to enjoy looking after her, get better soon, Fabia. I'm not happy to think of you in hospital. It makes me wish I was back there myself so that *I* could monitor you.'

Fabia smiled into the mouthpiece. 'That's my cue to once again remind you that you're wasted up there in the sky. But you don't want to hear it, do you?'

'You never know. If you keep saying it often enough I might start to believe it,' he countered. 'But enough about us. There's someone waiting to talk to you.' And Jessica's voice came chirping over the line.

In the midst of Fabia's relief there was the thought that if the culture proved that she had caught meningitis, how long would it be before she was free to take charge of her daughter again?

Bryce was already giving up his leave to look after Jessica, but he wouldn't be able to go on doing that indefinitely and the anxiety continued to hover.

The next day Fabia was beginning to feel better. The head pains were less severe, the gastric complications not so unpleasant. Obviously the antibiotics were starting to work and the results of the test were due any time.

Bryce had done as she'd asked and had kept away

for Jessica's sake. The two of them rang her frequently and their conversations were the bright moments in a long hospital day.

When the ward sister appeared at the side of her bed she was smiling, and Fabia raised herself up against the pillows expectantly.

'You're clear,' she said. 'It must have been some sort of stomach bug or a virus you've had. There were no signs of meningitis. You can go as soon as the doctor has seen you.'

'Oh! Thank goodness!' she breathed. 'I can't wait to get home to my family. I wouldn't let them visit, even though Bryce has been immunised against that sort of thing as he's a pilot flying to all sorts of hot spots. But there was the risk to my little girl.'

'I take it that Bryce is your husband?' the sister commented casually.

Fabia smiled.

'No. He's my brother-in-law.'

The other woman's eyes widened.

'Oh!'

When she'd gone Fabia lay back and savoured the moment. Soon she would be back with the two people she loved most in the world, and as she reached out for the bedside phone to tell Bryce the good news she was praying that he wouldn't do or say anything to take away the magic of the moment.

He didn't.

'That's wonderful news,' he said. 'I'd better get the place tidy. How soon can we come and pick you up?'

'I have to see the doctor first. I'll ring you as soon as he's confirmed that I'm being discharged. And, Bryce...'

'What?'

'Don't bother about the tidying up. Just be there. Jess and you are all the family I've got. When I became ill I thought she might have to go into care, and I'll never forget the horror of those moments before you turned up at the hospital.'

'Well, it's all over now,' he said soothingly. 'You're clear of that dreadful bug. Everything will soon be back to normal. You'll be able to take up where you left off.'

Fabia was wishing she could see his expression. He hadn't said 'we' can take up where 'we' left off. Yet did she want that. Before she'd been taken ill they'd been like distant strangers.

Surely after this they would be closer. She would bless him for evermore for being there for them in a crisis, but supposing that was all Bryce had seen it as? Would his defences be back in place now that it was over? She hoped not.

They left the hospital with Bryce carrying her case and Jessica skipping along between them. Quite unaware that what could have been an upsetting time in her young life was now safely over, she was chattering happily, and as Fabia's glance met his above her daughter's head the sun had never seemed brighter or the moment more welcome.

'I hope that all your leave hasn't been swallowed up, looking after Jessica and myself,' she said, feeling suddenly awkward.

Bryce shook his head. 'No. I've still got a couple of days left and if your tests had been positive I would have applied for an extension.'

Fabia wasn't the only one relieved at the outcome, he was thinking. He'd been devastated when he'd rung the centre and had been told by Giles that they suspected Fabia had caught meningitis.

Whatever else he might feel about Fabia, one thing was for sure—she brought out all his protective instincts. He couldn't forget for a moment the years that she'd had to struggle alone after Nick's death. Years when he could have helped if he'd known.

But he'd been more concerned about his own hurts than hers. Determined to put the old life behind him. Not caring what happened to the other innocent victim of the tragedy. And now he wanted to make up for it.

That was the essence of it, he kept telling himself. It was nothing to do with the fact that she was always in his thoughts.

Would he feel the same if Jessica wasn't around? he questioned, and knew the answer. The little one wasn't essentially the cause of his concern. She was the bonus that came with having Fabia back in his life.

So what was he going to do about it? Carry on with this slow progression to what might eventually turn out to be the beginning of a wonderful new life if only she would stop pining for this other fellow, or give in to an overwhelming longing and sweep her off her feet?

He knew what he wanted to do, but incredibly they'd already blended once in a moment of passionate tenderness and where had it got them? He'd backed off the moment it had been over. Not because it hadn't been magical, but because of who she was. And until he was sure he could accept that, it seemed as if the slow way was going to be the safest.

If she'd known what he was thinking, Fabia might have thought the day had lost its brightness. But with head bent she was listening to what Jessica had to say and didn't pick up on his thoughtful expression.

CHAPTER SEVEN

FOR the rest of the day Fabia was totally happy. She was home once more with Jessica, and Bryce was there, too. For how long she didn't know, but he wasn't showing any signs of leaving them yet, though he must have things to do. So, they were a precious threesome for a little while longer.

Maggie came round in the early evening to see how she was while Bryce and Jessica were out in the garden. And Fabia's neighbour said wonderingly. 'That man is something else. Do you know he'd been planning to go on holiday to the Seychelles for the last week of his leave and cancelled it when you became ill? You must be high up on his list of special people.'

'No. I didn't know,' Fabia said slowly, 'and it makes me feel dreadful. He never said.'

'Well, he wouldn't, would he? You would have been in a worse state than you were already if you'd known. The competition came round one afternoon and protested somewhat, which made me wonder if she was part of the cancelled holiday package.'

'The competition?'

'A slim blonde, not as wide across as a kipper and just as flat.'

Under other circumstances she might have laughed at Maggie's description of the glamorous flight purser, but not now.

'That sounds like Willow Martin,' Fabia said hollowly. 'She works for the same airline.'

'I shouldn't worry,' Maggie said consolingly. 'It's plain to see that Bryce is where he wants to be. He's entranced with Jessica.'

'Yes,' Fabia agreed absently as she digested the news that Willow had been to the house in an annoyed state and that Bryce had cancelled a holiday because of her own predicament.

And that wasn't the only cause of the sudden feeling of joylessness. Maggie had seen it, too, his devotion to Jess. Perhaps if it hadn't been for her daughter he wouldn't have been so keen to lend his support when she'd become ill.

Yet she knew him better than that. And she couldn't be jealous of her own child.

When Jessica was asleep and they were seated side by side on the sofa in the sitting room, she told him what Maggie had said.

'Why didn't you tell me that you'd made plans to go on holiday when I started to be ill?' she asked. 'You know I wouldn't have wanted you to cancel them.'

'Ah! You've been talking to Maggie.'

'Yes. She said that Willow came round to protest. Was she part of the holiday package?'

'No. She was not! I was going alone. Willow was merely trying to look after my interests. I've known her quite some time. She knows what Tiffany did to me and—'

'Thinks you're asking for trouble, getting involved with me.'

'Yes. Something like that.'

'So why did you stay?'

She was sounding ungrateful and knew it, but something was driving her on.

He was on his feet now and as Fabia watched the domestic bliss that she'd been so enjoying fly out of the window he said grittily, 'Do you honestly think I would leave you in the state you were in, with a suspected serious disease and no one to care for your daughter? I've been to the Seychelles before and will probably go again. So stop making a big thing out of me cancelling a holiday…and stop going on about Willow. She's a friend. No more, no less. And if you feel well enough to cope during the night, I'll be making tracks. I have an important appointment in the morning but I'll be in touch later in the day.'

Still on the offensive, she persisted. 'And what would you have done about that if I'd still been in hospital?'

'Cancelled it, of course.'

Bending, he brushed her cheek with his lips, and immediately she was contrite. Her arms went out to him, but he was backing away and telling her, 'If you need me for anything phone me. Otherwise, until tomorrow.' And with that he went.

Fabia was left with plenty of food for thought and none of it was appetising. In the first instance she'd been piqued because of Bryce's devotion to Jessica and ought to be ashamed of herself. Secondly, she'd been jealous of Willow, a woman she hardly knew and, thirdly and most importantly, Bryce had given his reasons for looking after them as the kind of thing he would do for anyone.

So Maggie's assumption that she was special to him was a bad guess. Jessica, yes, because *she* didn't pose any problem, but with regard to herself there would always be that lingering doubt.

*   *   *

As he lay sleepless later that night, Bryce's thoughts were racing. He didn't blame Fabia for getting up-tight. For one thing, she'd had a stressful few days and was only just getting over it.

Finding out that he'd cancelled a holiday had made her feel bad, but surely she realised that it wasn't the end of the world. The Seychelles would always be there, while she might not.

He supposed finding out that Willow had been round hadn't helped matters. He would have preferred it not to have happened himself but, having been in-volved in two failed marriages, Willow saw herself as an expert when it came to the pitfalls in a rela-tionship and had said a few times that of all the women in the world, why did he have to get involved with his dead wife's sister?

'You could have any woman you wanted,' she'd said to him on one occasion. 'Me included. So why go for someone who brings back memories…and comes with baggage?'

'I don't see Jessica as ''baggage'',' he'd told her tightly, but for the rest of it he hadn't had an answer. There was just something about Fabia that was getting to him and tomorrow he was going to take the first step towards doing something about it.

It would have been easy enough to tell her what he was planning during their exchange of words earlier. It might have made her feel better. But it would be time enough when he had something definite to say, and if it still didn't make any difference, if she still insisted she was in love with someone else, then he would have to rethink his motives.

*   *   *

Fabia returned to the centre the following Monday, which coincided with Jessica's first day back at school after the long summer break. She was excited at the thought of a new class and a new teacher and had chattered non-stop as she'd eaten her breakfast.

Fabia had observed her fondly. She'd always been a happy and uncomplicated child in spite of their circumstances, and since Bryce had appeared on the scene she had positively blossomed.

He'd rung in the late afternoon of the day after her discharge from hospital and there'd been no mention of him having kept the appointment that he'd referred to the previous day.

Fabia would have liked to have asked him what it had been connected with as she'd sensed its importance, but had decided that if he wanted her to know he would tell her.

'My leave is up at five o'clock this evening,' he told her. 'I'm on a flight to Toronto. But before I report back for duty I want to know how you're feeling.'

'Much better,' she told him truthfully. 'Whatever it was I picked up seems to have run its course. I'm reporting back for duty on Monday.'

He didn't comment on that but said instead, 'Monday is Jessica's first day back at school, isn't it? Tell her I'll be thinking of her.'

'Yes, I will,' she promised, not sure whether to be pleased or sorry that she was still a poor second on his list of priorities.

They chatted about minor things for a few moments longer and then he said that he had to go and get ready for the flight, which made her think glumly that they were back to square one—polite acquaintances.

'Take care, Bryce,' she said quickly, before he could ring off. 'Flying is dangerous these days.'

He laughed.

'So is crossing the road.' And added more seriously, 'If ever anything did happen to me, my will and all the relevant papers are with my bank. And, Fabia...'

'What?'

'You'd find a letter for you amongst them.'

Her face had twisted. 'Telling me all the things you can't or won't say to my face?'

'Maybe. Or it might be to inform you that I've left everything to Jessica.'

'Oh, no!' she breathed.

'Oh, yes,' he parried. 'I need to do something to make up for all the time you were left to cope alone.'

'But, Bryce, we weren't your responsibility then and we aren't now. You might decide to get married and you would owe it to your wife to provide for her, rather than some child she wouldn't even know.'

She heard him sigh.

'Will you, please, let me be the overseer of my own affairs, Fabia? I am expecting to live to a ripe old age. These are merely eventualities that we're discussing and I'm not prepared to argue about them. And now I do have to go. I'll see you around.'

That had been it. No fuss. No arrangements for him to visit them in the near future.

When she appeared at the door of his office Giles looked up and his smile told her that he was glad to see her back. 'We've missed you,' he said, and her spirits lifted. It was nice to know that she registered with someone.

The other nurses crowded around as she hung up her coat, asking just how bad the illness had been and commenting that she'd had a lucky escape. They were all only too aware that the risk of infection was part of the job.

'It could have been worse,' she told them. 'The thing that really got to me was the thought of being away from Jessica, but a friend stepped in and looked after her for me.'

Most of them had seen Bryce at one time or another when he'd called at the centre, but none of them knew just what their relationship was, and she wasn't going to enlighten them by explaining that it was he who'd come to the rescue. Especially now that the brief closeness they'd shared was wearing off.

It was still a source of amazement to her that they'd once almost made love. It was as if it had been in another lifetime. She'd thought it might be the beginning of something very special between them, but it had turned out to be just a one-off.

She knew that lots of couples slept together on short acquaintance but theirs wouldn't have been like that. They'd known each other a long time and yet, incredibly, after the first few moments in each other's arms, it had been as if they didn't know each other at all.

As usual, the airport was a seething hive of activity and it was inevitable that some of those passing through should find their way to the walk-in centre, but the last person Fabia was expecting to be confronted with in the middle of the morning was Guy Forrester.

'Hi, there, Fabia,' he said as she observed him, open-mouthed, 'You look surprised.'

'I am,' she told him. 'You're the last person I would expect to see here. You're miles away from Cornwall. What brings you to my patch?'

Guy smiled. 'Your irresistible charms.'

'I doubt it,' she commented drily. 'How about the truth?'

'I'm leaving the studio behind for a few months and doing a round-the-world trip. I couldn't get the flight I wanted from an airport nearer home, so here I am. I don't fly out until late afternoon, so can we have lunch?'

'Only a very quick snack,' she told him, 'as I have to pick Jessica up from school.'

'What time do you finish?'

'Half past one.'

'I'll be waiting for you in the snack bar across the way then. OK?'

'Er...yes,' she agreed, still bemused by his appearance.

It was ironic. She'd had one eye on the door all morning, hoping that Bryce might appear, but instead Guy had turned up. If he was thinking that she might be more likely to warm to him on her own territory, he was mistaken.

Yet he was hardly likely to be wanting to pursue their acquaintance to any length if he was off on a trip round the world, she told herself, and it was good to see him again. The painting he'd done of her had been a nice gesture, and at the first opportunity she intended to have it framed.

'So tell me what you've been up to,' he said when she joined him in the eaterie opposite the centre.

'Nothing exciting, I'm afraid,' she told him. 'I spent three days in hospital last week being tested and treated for suspected meningitis, which prompts me to ask if you've had all your vaccinations.'

'Yes. I've had the lot,' he replied promptly. 'I've been planning this trip for a long while. Pity you couldn't have come with me.'

'I do happen to have a small daughter and a job to hold down,' she told him laughingly. 'If you want female companionship, look for a girl who's got no responsibilities.'

He reached across and, taking her hand in his, looked deep into her eyes.

'Would you have come otherwise?'

She was still smiling. Guy was something else. She'd like to bet that all this was on the spur of the moment. The first attractive woman he came across in his wanderings would blot out any yearnings he might have regarding herself.

'Of course not. You're not my type,' she told him, still smiling and letting her hand stay in his.

'It's Hollister with you, isn't it?' he said whimsically. 'Every time.'

Fabia nodded.

'I've loved Bryce for as long as I can remember.'

Guy sighed.

'So why doesn't he do something about it? It's clear he feels the same. He wasn't pleased when I was hanging around in Cornwall. Surely he knows how you feel.'

'It's not that simple, Guy. Bryce was married to my sister who was frivolous, pleasure-loving…and very beautiful. He was a doctor in those days and I guess she was bored with the life as he worked long hours and often came home exhausted.

'She and my husband began an affair. They'd

planned to go away together, but on the way to the airport they were involved in a car crash and both were killed.'

It was Guy's turn to be taken aback.

'Good grief! What a ghastly mess.'

'Yes, it was. Still is as far as Bryce is concerned.'

'But why take it out on you?'

'He doesn't. Not in the true sense anyway. But the past hardly makes for a stress-free relationship between us.'

At that moment his flight was called and, releasing her hand, he got to his feet.

'Must go, Fabia. Thought it was worth one more try, but I get the picture now. Hope that you and Hollister sort things out soon.'

When he'd gone she sat staring into space. Guy was an uncomplicated soul but he was all on the surface. She didn't think there was much depth to him…and as to his parting shot, maybe it was time that she did something about the stalemate situation that she and Bryce were in. She wasn't to know that it had just worsened.

It was one of those days, Bryce was thinking as he made his way towards the walk-in centre. Maybe a glimpse of Fabia would put things right if she hadn't already left for home.

There'd been an unpleasant incident on the flight he'd just made which had left him seething. A passenger had produced a mobile phone and had shown every sign of using it just as they'd begun the landing process.

He was a foreign national and had tried to pretend a language problem when the cabin crew had remonstrated with him. It had ended in a scuffle as they'd tried to take the phone off him, which had resulted in the staff not being in their seats as the plane had come in to land and an overhead luggage compartment was still open.

The man's stupidity was unpardonable, his lack of concern for others incredible, as passengers were constantly warned that the use of mobile phones was prohibited. He'd been heard speaking fluent English by the cabin crew prior to the incident, and as far as they were concerned had been deliberately causing trouble.

When Bryce and his co-pilot had heard what had been going on, it had been too late to abandon touchdown.

It hadn't been the worst thing that had ever happened to him on a flight, but it hadn't been the best either, and he'd made sure that when they had safely landed the police had been waiting to arrest the culprit.

As he was about to go into the centre, he glanced into the snack bar across the way and stopped in his tracks, unable to believe his eyes.

Fabia and the artist were in there, holding hands across the table as they looked into each other's eyes. So he hadn't been wrong about him, There *was* something going on between them.

His anger over the incident on the aircraft was wiped out by a feeling of sick disbelief. Why hadn't she told him that she preferred Forrester? Yet why should she? He had no claim on her, had he?

And whose fault was that? he asked himself as he began to retrace his steps. He'd been dithering like a flustered schoolboy for weeks and now had left it too late. It looked as if she'd finally given up on the mystery man and fallen for Forrester.

As he drove the short distance home he was visualising Jessica with the artist, and they were not happy thoughts. Surely Fabia would take her daughter's feelings into consideration before making any commitment to Forrester? But they'd looked like a couple in love and reason didn't always prevail when romance was in the air.

He supposed he was a decent enough man, but Forrester was a womaniser. He'd seen him chatting up women on the seafront and in the pub at St Ives at the same time as he'd been sniffing round Fabia. He couldn't bear the thought of her being hurt again. That was one of the reasons why he'd held back for so long.

Stay away from her, he told himself as he unlocked the door of the empty house. You had your chance and you've blown it.

In the days that followed he did just that…stayed away…and it left him with the feeling that the hours were just something to be got through.

But it was a decision he'd made and was determined to stick to. He'd been crazy to think that he and Fabia could have made a go of it after their past history.

There was another decision pending and, although less painful, it wasn't going to be an easy one to make. But it could wait a while. There was no immediate urgency. In fact, ever since he'd seen Fabia with Forrester there'd seemed to be no urgency about anything in his life.

Since that first day when he'd walked into the cen-

tre and seen what for a crazy moment he'd thought
had been Tiffany, his life hadn't been the same. He'd
actually been happy, carefree even, and it had all been
because of a slender, golden-haired nurse and a child.

He'd allowed himself to love Jessica because she
was sweet and innocent, and as he'd got to know
Fabia all over again, he'd found her to be the same.
And what had he done about it? Nothing, except kiss
her passionately and then cast the paradise he'd
glimpsed to one side.

As the days went by with no word from Bryce, Fabia
felt gloom descend. Where was he? she wondered.
On long stopovers? Or was he ill, with no one to care
for him? It would be awful if that were the case after
he'd been so supportive when she'd had the virus.

Yet he had her number. All he had to do was ring
and she would be there if he needed her.

There could be another reason for his silence and
she had a sinking feeling that it might be the real one.
He was easing himself away from them, after deciding that getting too close wasn't a good idea.

If that was the case, it wasn't fair to Jessica, she
told herself. She kept asking where he was. Bryce had
no right to be there for the child one moment and
gone the next. Better that he'd never been there at all
than this.

At last she could stand it no longer and, having
discovered that he was on a midday flight to New
York, she waylaid him in the airport.

He was always something to see in his uniform,
but she thought that today he looked tired and grim-
faced when she confronted him.

'Fabia,' he said unsmilingly. 'What can I do for you?'

'You can tell me why you've not been in touch,' she said quietly, having no wish to be overheard. 'I've been wondering if you were ill. Or if something bad had happened.'

'No. I'm fine,' he said tonelessly. 'I've just been rather busy. Er…how's Jessica?'

'Missing you…and so am I. Have I done something to offend you?'

'No, of course not,' he said in the same flat monotone. 'But I do have other things going on in my life.'

'I get the message. Jess and I are being hung out to dry for some reason that I don't understand.'

'Think that if you must, but I have to go. I have a plane to fly.'

As he walked away the set of his shoulders was just as much a reproof as the cold blue gaze he'd bestowed upon her, and as she went despondently to find her car there was a certainty in her that this was how it was going to be from now on. But why?

The mornings were cold and crisp. Autumn had arrived and with it came a melancholy born not only from the departure of sunny days and light nights.

When Fabia saw herself in the mirror it was a white face with lacklustre eyes and a sad mouth that looked back at her. She put on a cheerful show for Jessica, but the moment she was alone the dejection took over.

She wished sometimes that Bryce had never come back into her life. At least she'd had a degree of contentment before, but now it was all 'if onlys' and 'maybes'.

It was cruel, what he'd done to them. Bringing light into their lives and then leaving them in shadow. If this was what he was like, they were better off without him, she told herself frequently. Yet there had to be a reason. She'd known and respected him too long to accept what he was doing without question.

But she couldn't face the thought of another bleak encounter like their last meeting. If there was to be any change in the atmosphere it had to come from him because so far as she knew she'd done nothing wrong.

Jessica was still asking after Bryce but not as often. It was her birthday soon and Fabia wondered if he would remember and, if he did, what he would do about it.

It was on a Saturday and she was having a party with two girl friends from school and the boys next door. It was her one topic of conversation at the moment and Fabia prayed that nothing would happen to spoil her day.

The children were coming for lunch and in the afternoon she intended taking the five of them to the travelling fair that was coming to the village for the weekend.

When the day dawned Fabia watched her daughter open her presents with a familiar ache inside her. Most of the gift-wrapped packages were from herself because they had no family to share the day with.

She'd given up on Bryce. There'd been no word from him and it really hurt that the sins of long ago should be reaching out to touch her daughter, but, oblivious to everything but the moment, Jessica seemed happy enough.

Still in her pyjamas, she was seated on one of the

wide window-seats, surrounded by wrapping and la-
bels as she hugged one of the soft toys that had been
in the packages.

At that moment she lifted her head and Fabia saw
her face light up. In a flash she was jumping down
and running towards the door crying, 'He's here.
Uncle Bryce is here!'

When Fabia went to the window he was getting out
of the car, and in that moment she forgave him everything. Whatever was wrong between the two of
them, he'd remembered Jessica.

By the time she got to the door they were coming
down the path together hand in hand.

'I've got something in the boot of my car for this
young lady,' he said as their glances met. Turning to
the excited child, he said, 'Close your eyes, Jessica.'

To Fabia he said in a low voice. 'I hope she hasn't
got a doll's pram.'

She shook her head.

'Good.'

He could have found that out by ringing her first,
she thought, but it wasn't the moment for letting any
minor niggle out into the open.

'So how have you been?' he asked a little later as
they watched Jessica tucking up her dolls in the new
pram.

'Fine,' she lied. 'And you?'

'The same, though very busy.'

This is awful, she was thinking. Was this the man
she loved? The same one who'd kissed her on that
never-to-be-forgotten night? But it was her daughter's
birthday. Not the right time for soul-searching between them. In any case, if their last meeting was
anything to go by, he would have nothing to say.

'How long can you stay?' she asked. 'Jessica has missed you. We're having a little party at lunchtime with four of her friends and then going to the village fair this afternoon.'

'And I'm invited?'

'Yes, of course. Why should you think otherwise?'

'It might be because you're expecting someone else and two's company and three's a crowd.'

'We're talking about seven of us, not two,' she replied, puzzled by the comment.

'Yes, we are, aren't we?' he agreed. 'Of course I'll stay if that will make her happy.'

So it looked as if Forrester wasn't going to be around for the party, Bryce thought bleakly. Cornwall was a long way off, yet he'd made it to the airport that day. Every time he thought about them holding hands over the table in the snack bar, he felt sick. Fabia might have told him, had the decency to let him know that she and the artist were more than friends. Was he never to get the truth from the women in his life?

He put his sombre thoughts to one side for the party, and as he laughed and played with the children anyone not aware of their relationship would have thought him a fond father entertaining his daughter and her friends.

Fabia watched him thoughtfully. Something was bugging him. Had his comment about her expecting someone had anything to do with it?

Yet who else would she be expecting, for heaven's sake? Bryce knew that her circle of friends and acquaintances was limited, with a small child to bring up and her job at the airport.

As they strolled round the fair, Jessica hung onto

his hand tightly while Fabia shepherded the others around. When they all crowded onto a carousel with big wooden horses bobbing up and down he put Jessica on the one nearest to him and then helped Fabia to lift the others into place.

'You all right?' he asked as they waited for it to set off.

'Yes, thanks,' she said quietly.

He had made Jessica happy by turning up, but Fabia wasn't sure how she felt. She was grateful, of course. How could she be anything else if he'd brought joy to her daughter's special day? But for her own part she was miserable and confused and wished she could see into his mind.

There were a lot of people there, among them gangs of boisterous youths milling around the side-shows. As a group of them jostled past, one of them lurched against Fabia and sent her off balance.

Bryce reached out for her and as she steadied herself in his arms she looked up at him with the questions that plagued her mind in her eyes.

It was a long time since they'd been so close and he didn't want to let her go, but the lad turned back and was muttering an apology. Fabia assured him that there was no harm done and moved out of Bryce's hold.

She could have stayed there for ever but the children were pulling at them to move on, and the only time she wanted to be in Bryce's arms was when he wanted her there. Not when some clumsy lad had cat-apulted her into his embrace.

Watching his jaw tighten, she thought that he had some nerve. He hadn't been near her in weeks but had been ready to take advantage of the moment, and when she hadn't responded he hadn't liked it.

As they all walked back to the cottage in the winter twilight, she was wondering how much longer he would stay.

As if reading her mind, he said, 'I'll have to make tracks soon. I have a night flight.'

The children were running on ahead and for the first time they had a moment alone.

'Thanks for coming. You've made Jessica's day,' she said levelly. 'I'm glad you didn't punish her for whatever it is that I've done. If ever you want to spend some time with her without me being around, it's all right.'

Bryce groaned and, turning to her, said tersely. 'That's very kind of you, but are you sure you want me butting in?'

'Butting in? You wouldn't be doing that. I don't understand what you mean.'

'Think about it and you will.'

When they got back, the mothers of the children were waiting to collect them, and by the time Fabia and Jessica had waved them off Bryce was ready to leave, too.

'Would you like me to take you out some time?' he asked the child, swinging her up in his arms for a goodbye hug.

He knew it was a crazy thing to suggest. It would cause more pain for him in the long run, but the temptation was there.

'And Mummy, too?' she asked.

There was a pause. Not a long one, but long enough

for Fabia to know that wasn't what he'd meant. Yet whose fault was that? she asked herself. She was the one who'd suggested it.

'Yes, of course…if she wants to come,' he said.

CHAPTER EIGHT

LATER that night, in the cockpit beneath the stars, Bryce's thoughts were on the day that was almost past.

The welcome he'd received from Jessica had warmed his heart. If her mother had been less enthusiastic, he supposed the fact that Fabia was in a new relationship could account for that.

But why hadn't Forrester been there? There'd been no card or gift from him that he could see, and his name hadn't been mentioned by either mother or daughter.

He supposed he could have taken Jessica to one side and asked her about him, but he'd been damned if he was going to use an unsuspecting child to appease his curiosity. It was Fabia's place to tell him what was going on. They were supposed to be friends, for heaven's sake!

She'd got the message, though, knew he wasn't making any more moves in her direction. But why act as if she didn't know the reason?

He'd almost weakened when he'd held her for those brief moments at the fair, but that time it had been her turn to let him see that they weren't going anywhere.

His flight schedule for the next two weeks was going to be hectic, but once it had evened out he was going to take her up on the offer of seeing Jessica.

Whatever else she was up to, her generosity of

spirit hadn't disappeared with regard to that, but, much as he loved the child, it would be a poor substitute for the times they'd been a happy threesome.

Christmas was approaching and he guessed she and Forrester wouldn't want him around then, so if he was going to take Jessica anywhere, the sooner the better.

When Bryce rang two weeks later Jessica answered the phone.

'Mummy's in the shower,' she informed him when he asked to speak to Fabia.

'I see. Could you give her a message?'

'Yes,' she said obediently.

'Tell her that if it's convenient, I'll come for you on Saturday and take you to see a movie. Your choice.'

'Yes, please,' she whooped, then added as if having sudden doubts. 'You won't make her cry again, will you?'

'Cry? I've never made your mummy cry,' he said incredulously.

'It was when you'd gone home after my party. She was upset and couldn't stop crying.'

'That wouldn't have been anything to do with me,' he said gently as his mind registered what she was saying. 'I would never do anything to make her unhappy. It must have been because of something else.'

Did Jessica know about Forrester? he was wondering. Had Fabia's tears been because he'd not been there for her daughter's birthday?

'Tell her I'll be round at half past one on Saturday,' he said, before she could impart any more unsettling information. 'If it isn't convenient, ask her to give me a ring.'

*   *   *

It was true, what Jessica had told him. As she'd watched his car pull away on the evening of Jessica's birthday, all Fabia's pent-up misery had surfaced and the tears that hadn't been far from the surface all day had come.

It hadn't lasted long but it had been enough for Jessica to remember that it had been his name that Fabia had said over and over again between her sobs.

When he arrived at the cottage on Saturday, Jessica was next door with Maggie and her family. Before Fabia could go to fetch her he said, 'Hold on a second, Fabia. There's something I want to ask you.'

'Yes?'

'Jessica thinks that I was responsible for you being upset on the night of her party. Surely not. I thought I hadn't put a foot wrong.'

She looked at him in consternation.

'When did she tell you that?'

'The other day, when I phoned.'

'I *was* upset, yes, but Jess shouldn't have told you.'

She could feel her colour rising. This was a discussion she could do without.

'It wasn't connected with me, though?'

'Why would you think that?'

'I don't. It was Jessica who said I was to blame, and I wondered why she would say that.'

'I'm sure I have no idea,' she said coolly. 'We all have our dark days and that was one of mine.'

'But it was her birthday.'

'Yes. I know that, and I wasn't proud of myself for bringing the doldrums into her special day.'

'So are you going to tell me what was wrong?'

'I don't think you'd want to hear.'

She wasn't going to tell him that she'd wept because she was tired of waiting. Tired of living on hope, of being sidestepped whenever the mood took him and knowing he wasn't going to change.

'You're going to be late for the film if you don't get moving,' she reminded him. 'I'll go and fetch Jess.'

'Are you coming with us?'

'Do you want me to?'

Bryce sighed. 'Of course I do. Just as long as I won't be treading on anyone's toes.'

'Such as?'

He'd had enough. 'Your boyfriend.'

'And who might that be?'

'For heaven's sake, Fabia, why don't you come out in the open? I saw you and Forrester holding hands across from the walk-in centre.'

Fabia began to laugh but there was no mirth in it.

'So that's what it's all been about. You've been giving me the cold shoulder because you thought that Guy and I were—'

'In love? It certainly looked like it.'

'And you immediately thought that deceit runs in my family. I can't believe you've shunned me all this time because of that.'

'What was I supposed to think?' he snapped. 'I was on my way to see you and there you were, gazing into each other's eyes.'

'It's a pity you're not into lipreading,' she told him quietly. 'If you were, you might have seen that I was telling him that he wasn't my type. Guy was off on a round-the-world trip and called to see me before his flight. He was flirting with me, yes, but it was more to kill time than anything else.

'So, you see, you've made us both miserable for nothing. But it won't happen again. From now on I'm going to be immune from your mood swings. You don't trust me, Bryce. You never will. I'll give the film a miss if it's all the same to you.'

Sitting beside a wide-eyed Jessica in the darkened cinema, Bryce was coming to terms with the latest backslide in his relationship with Fabia.

There was relief in him because Forrester wasn't part of her life, but it was far outweighed by dismay. He didn't blame her for being angry. A man with less stupid pride than himself would have brought it out into the open right at the beginning when he'd first seen Fabia and the artist together, but not he. He'd sulked behind a barrier of prejudgement and the tender shoots of what might have been had withered in the process.

When he took Jessica home after the film Fabia met them at the door and there was no invitation for him to enter, just a polite word of thanks. And because he knew he deserved it, he didn't protest.

There'd been a spate of crushed toes from dropped luggage and sprained backs from carrying it during the days that followed, and most of them had found their way to the centre.

A member of the maintenance staff had been in for treatment after oil had splashed into his eyes and an elderly man who'd thought he'd missed his plane had been brought to them with a suspected heart attack.

All part of a day's work for the nurses of the centre, and for Fabia something to take her mind off the confrontation with Bryce the previous weekend.

She still couldn't believe that he could be so blind as not to see that he was the one she cared for. It was unfortunate that he had seen her with Guy that day, but why, for goodness' sake, hadn't he mentioned it? It would have cleared the air immediately, instead of causing an estrangement that had led to miserable days and nights.

He'd done her one favour, though. Made her see beyond doubt that they were on different wavelengths. She couldn't take any more of it. Better to be as she'd been before he'd come back on the scene than in a state of fraught suspense all the time, she told herself.

He hadn't been near since they'd said their strained goodbyes on her doorstep, and whenever she questioned if she'd been too harsh she always came back to the same answer—that it was better this way.

Except that out of sight didn't mean out of mind. Fabia thought of him constantly, praying that one day he would let go of the past and be happy.

And in the meantime, during the dark days of November, she involved herself in lukewarm preparations for the coming festive season.

On a grey early morning a month before Christmas, there was a serious incident at the airport.

Fabia had only just arrived at the centre when pandemonium broke loose.

'There's been a crash landing on a flight from Spain,' Giles told his staff. 'We're needed out there on the tarmac.'

As the nurses hurried towards the runway, the airport's fire services were already racing to the scene and ambulances from nearby depots were being alerted.

A detaining hand from behind brought Fabia to a halt. When she turned, Willow was there, her face tense in the breaking dawn.

'It's Bryce's flight,' she said.

'Oh, no!' Fabia cried as fear gripped her heart. 'How bad is it?'

The other woman shook her head.

'I don't know. I should have been on it, but my schedule was changed at the last minute.'

They were running side by side now and Fabia was thinking that if anything had happened to him she would never have told him she loved him. It would be the final chapter of a sad story that had started long ago.

At the point of landing, one of the wings had dipped, scraping the ground and making deep furrows in the tarmac, and now the plane was leaning crazily at a thirty-degree angle. In the glare of floodlights Fabia could see that the undercarriage on the same side as the dipped wing was crumpled and collapsed.

The emergency chutes were already in place and passengers were being helped onto them by the crew. It was a scene out of a nightmare and as Fabia and the other nurse waited for them at the bottom, there was no one more traumatised than herself because Bryce was involved and so far there was no sign of him.

Fire risk was always a hazard in such circumstances and the fire crews were spreading foam along the runway lest spilt fuel resulted in an inferno.

As the crew followed the escaping passengers down the chute, a purser gasped. 'The co-pilot has collapsed. The captain thinks it's his heart. He's not sure how he's going to get him down the chute. I offered to stay behind but he wouldn't let me.'

'He needs to get him out of there fast,' the fire chief said tightly. 'It could go up any moment. The emergency services will sort the co-pilot out once they're down here.'

'Captain Hollister is also a doctor of many years' experience,' Fabia told him raggedly as she helped a bewildered elderly woman off the chute. 'He knows what he's doing.'

The purser was eyeing her in surprise.

'You know him?'

'Yes,' she said briefly. 'We worked together a long time ago.'

There were plenty of cuts and bruises to be seen to amongst the passengers but at first glance no serious injuries, and now ambulances were arriving from the surrounding areas to assist the nurses from the centre.

In view of the seriousness of the incident, it was miraculous that no one had been hurt more seriously, Fabia thought, but where was Bryce? If the plane did catch fire, he and the other officer wouldn't stand a chance. Her blood was running cold with the horror of it. She couldn't go home to Jessica with the dreadful tidings that he was gone for ever out of their lives.

It seemed like an eternity, yet it could only have been minutes, before a shout went up. When Fabia raised her head from the casualty she was attending she saw they were there, at the top of the chute—two uniformed figures, with Bryce supporting the other man.

As they came down he held onto the limp figure tightly, and the moment they reached the bottom she heard him tell the paramedics calmly, 'We have a cardiac arrest here. I've resuscitated the best I could under the circumstances, and he's breathing again. It's up to you guys now.'

It was his tone of voice that broke down her own composure, such as it was. How could he be so cool? Didn't he know that she'd just gone through torment? But he didn't know, did he? She was always the anguished bystander where he was concerned, and today had been in a class of its own.

As the man she'd been treating was taken away by a member of one of the ambulance crews, Fabia thought that amazingly in just a matter of minutes it was all under control. The passengers needing to be checked over had been taken to hospital and Bryce was watching them load the stretcher with his sick colleague on it into a waiting ambulance.

The only thing out of control were her feelings. In the blessed relief of seeing Bryce safe she needed him to hold her, to reassure her that it was all right between them, that the future was theirs. But she knew it would never work out like that.

Her pent-up anxiety was turning to tears and, with shoulders shaking, she stood to one side, away from the view of the crowd.

As the doors of the ambulance closed on his co-pilot, Bryce's thoughts turned to Fabia. The nurses from the centre would have been the first on the spot at an incident like this. He could see flashes of blue uniform moving amongst those present, but none of them belonged to her.

A voice at his elbow had him turning quickly, but it was a pale-faced Willow beside him.

'If you're looking for Fabia, she's over there, breaking her heart,' she said. 'I wouldn't be surprised if it isn't connected with you. You frightened the life out of us. Even my legs are like jelly. So how Fabia is feeling I wouldn't like to guess. When I told her it was your flight that was in crisis, she was devastated.'

He was already striding off, calling over his shoulder, 'Thanks, Willow. I'll be seeing you.'

When she felt a touch on her shoulder, Fabia turned slowly. Her face was blotched, her eyes brimming, and her sobs increased when she saw who it was.

Bryce held out a clean white handkerchief and she took it from him without speaking.

'What's wrong, Fabia?' he asked gently. 'It's over. Thankfully, we made it. I know that poor old Jack hasn't come out of it very well, but he'll get the best possible care once they've admitted him to the cardiac unit.'

'I thought I was going to lose you,' she sobbed, 'without you ever knowing…'

Her voice trailed away and he reached out for her and took her in his arms.

'Without me knowing what?' he murmured with his mouth against the bright swathe of her hair.

'That I love you. I always have.'

Fabia felt him tense. His hold on her tightened.

'So it is me,' he breathed. 'I'm the one who has never returned your feelings. I did wonder, but the idea seemed absurd and I put it out of my head. How could I have been so blind, though? How long have you felt like this, Fabia?'

'For as long as I can remember,' she said, miserably aware that the news hadn't transported him into the realms of delight. 'Can we drop the subject? If I hadn't been so overwrought, I wouldn't have said anything.'

She was calm now, her tears drying as she thought dismally that this was like a repeat of the night they'd let passion take over. He'd turned that into a joyless moment, too.

'We have to talk. I'll come round tonight if that's all right with you,' he was saying. He touched her cheek gently. 'In the meantime, promise me—no more tears.'

Giles was hovering. She could see him out of the corner of her eye.

'I have to go,' she told Bryce. 'We're due back at the centre.'

He nodded, his arms falling away.

'So I'll see you tonight?'

'Yes. I suppose so,' she agreed listlessly.

It was clear that the earth hadn't moved for him when she'd made her tearful confession, so what would there be to talk about when he came round that evening?

Air accident investigation officers had arrived on the scene almost immediately. Maintenance records showed there had been some recent work on the undercarriage, and if it hadn't been completed satisfactorily the locking procedure could have failed. Alternatively, there could have been a fault in the cockpit signals.

Evidence from Bryce and his crew would give them the clearest picture of what had happened, but for now they'd all been debriefed and sent home to rest until such time as they were called upon to assist the investigation. But for the man who had landed the aircraft safely under dangerous conditions, rest was the last thing he was contemplating.

Bryce wanted to see for himself how his co-pilot was. Jack Telfer was a friend as well as a colleague. As far as he knew, the forty-five-year-old had never had a day's illness in his life, but of late there'd been stress in his personal life and he'd been burning himself out because of it.

But more than that, Bryce needed time to think about what Fabia had told him when she'd wept in his arms on the tarmac that chill November morning.

He was still reeling. She was beautiful and desirable and she loved him. But which of the two Bryce Hollisters was she in love with? The trusting, uncomplicated surgeon of the past, or the wary pilot he'd become? And would it be fair to inflict the latter on her?

There was something else on his mind, too. A decision he'd made that he didn't want to back down on, which could complicate matters even further. But that would have to wait.

As she waited for Bryce that night, Fabia felt there was nothing to talk about. If Bryce loved her, he would have done something about it there and then at the airport. But instead he'd bombarded her with questions instead of kisses and now she was wishing that they'd left it at that. She'd already said her piece.

Jessica was asleep so there would be just the two of them playing out a charade. What would he do? Let her down lightly? Tell her he appreciated being the object of her affections but that once bitten was twice shy?

Her timing had been atrocious. He'd just averted what could have been a terrible tragedy for passengers and crew and seen his co-pilot have a heart attack. On top of all that, she'd laid upon him the burden of her love. Maybe it wasn't surprising that Bryce hadn't gone away rejoicing.

Yet when he came he brought flowers, a florist's bouquet of cream roses, lily of the valley and golden rod. As she observed him wonderingly her spirits rose.

He looked tired. There were lines of fatigue around his eyes and he was paler than usual, but he was smiling as he stepped over the threshold and gave her the flowers.

'To make up for being such a moron this morning,' he explained.

Fabia felt her cheeks start to burn. Were the flowers just a peace offering, or did they mean something else?

Bryce was looking around him as he took off his jacket.

'Jessica asleep?' he questioned.

'Yes,' she told him. 'Are you disappointed?'

'No. Not on this occasion. I've been thinking non-stop about what you told me this morning, and I don't know what to say. I couldn't take it in at first, on top of what had just happened, but since then I've had time to let it sink in and have come to the conclusion that I don't deserve you, Fabia.'

So this was how it was going to be. No joyful coming together of like minds. No passionate responding to their physical needs. Just a calm discussion that was meant to let her off lightly.

Yet what had she expected? That their lives would change because she'd told Bryce she loved him?

'Surely I should be the judge of that,' she countered, with a steadiness that belied the chaos of her thoughts.

He smiled. 'Possibly. But whenever I feel the chemistry between us start to work, and we both know it's there, I begin to remember that you've already been badly hurt once and there is no way I would want to hurt you more.'

'Which is a roundabout way of saying that you're punishing me for what Tiffany did.'

'Of course not, never that. None of it was your fault. But we're going round in circles, What I came to say is this. Give me a little more time, Fabia. You and Jessica are very important to me. I treasure you both.'

'But?'

'But, as I've just said, I'm not sure that I can make you happy, and until I am, can't we be good friends? I've got the inquiry over today's averted catastrophe coming up, and I have something else big going on in my life at the moment, too. So, you see...'

'Yes, I see,' she said wearily. 'Let's be friends, by all means.'

Since Nick's death she'd never looked at another man until Bryce had come back into her life. With him it was different, so different that she'd told him she loved him, and where had it got her. She'd been gently but firmly put in her place and the chemistry that he'd referred to was about as far away as the clouds in the sky.

Until Bryce got to his feet and came to stand in front of her. As he looked down at her with concern in his bright blue gaze, rebellion suddenly sparked inside Fabia. Rising, she placed her arms around his neck and with a purpose that she wouldn't have believed herself capable of she brought his face level with hers and kissed him long and lingeringly.

After the first seconds of surprise Bryce responded as the hunger in them took over.

'You shouldn't have done that, Fabia,' he breathed when at last they drew apart. 'How can I think straight when my loins ache to make love to you?'

She smiled. 'Thinking straight comes easier to you than it does to me,' she said easily. 'You'll cope.' And walking across the room, she opened the door and waited for him to leave.

He had one last thing to say and she didn't know whether to draw comfort from it or take it to be another warning that they weren't going anywhere.

'Better to be passionate friends, Fabia, than ill-fated lovers.'

In the weeks up to Christmas Fabia wondered what Bryce had planned. He was unpredictable in some ways but very predictable in others.

Would he go down to Cornwall for the Christmas break? she wondered. Hit the high spots of London? Or spend the two days of festivities locally?

He'd called in to see her a couple of times at the centre, but on each occasion she'd been treating someone and they'd had no time to talk.

The first time she had been with a pregnant woman who had had severe stomach pains and bleeding on the way to the airport. She was three months pregnant with her first baby and the possibility of a miscarriage was likely. It had meant the end of holiday plans for the young couple and a trip to hospital.

On the second occasion it had been a youth who'd been drinking heavily prior to flying to New York. There'd been some rowdyism in the departure lounge amongst the group he was with, and he'd fallen and cut himself.

'I'll call round tonight,' Bryce had said as she'd directed the lad into the consulting room.

She'd nodded. 'Yes, please, do. I've phoned a few times but must have picked the wrong moments.'

Fabia wanted to ask him how the inquiry into the crash-landing was going, and what he was doing for Christmas. She didn't want to invite him to spend it with Jessica and herself if he had other, more exciting plans.

It was a strange state of affairs. After the night when he'd called to tell her in a roundabout sort of way that he wasn't ready for commitment, and she'd been driven to do something to protest at his aggravating reasoning, there'd been no further differences between them. But neither had there been any contact.

Fabia thought sometimes that if she'd been more provocative and more outreaching he might have thought more of her. But that was what Tiffany had been like and, added to that, she had her pride.

Although it hadn't been much in evidence on the day when she'd sobbed in his arms and told him she loved him. Yet it had cleared the air. If *his* feelings were kept behind closed doors, *hers* weren't any more.

When he'd left the cottage that night, Bryce had been sorely tempted to turn back. What was the matter with him? he'd thought. Telling her he wanted them to be friends and that he didn't deserve her love when the mere sight of her set his pulses racing. Any other man would have jumped at the chance of having someone like Fabia in love with him.

The moment she'd touched him it had been there as it always was, passion, tenderness, need. Yet for some stupid reason of his own he hadn't grasped the opportunity.

He'd smiled a grim smile. What had he been worrying about? That Fabia would turn out to be the same as her sister? He knew better than that now. She was everything that Tiffany hadn't been, but he still couldn't help wishing that there was no family connection.

When she'd told him with a sort of simple dignity that she loved him and had done for a long time, in the middle of his amazement he'd felt blessed, as if something sweet and sacred had come into his blighted life. Maybe that was why he felt that he didn't deserve her.

As he'd turned onto the driveway of his house he'd thought with a sudden lifting of spirits that they had plenty of time to find their way.

He'd been jealous of the two men in her life. But she'd soon put his mind at rest about the artist and, incredibly, he'd discovered that he was the man she'd loved in vain for so long. So both those spectres had been banished.

If Fabia's expression was guarded when she opened the door to him one evening, Jessica's cry of delight made up for it.

'And so what's Father Christmas bringing?' he

asked as he scooped her up in his arms. Their eyes met over Jessica's head and Fabia said with a quizzical smile, 'It's more like what isn't he bringing.'

'I'd like to get involved,' he told her in a low voice. 'Any ideas?'

'Mmm. Later maybe.'

The sight of him was warming her heart. With the casual elegance that was so much a part of him, he was dressed in a blue cashmere sweater and jeans. In anyone's language, a man to be noticed.

'Have you been told the findings of the inquiry yet?' she asked when Jessica had calmed down.

'No. But it seems pretty clear from all accounts that there was a fault in the undercarriage so someone in Maintenance is going to be in big trouble.'

'You could have been killed,' she said sombrely.

'Yes, I know, and so could a lot of other people, but as long as the world exists there will be human error. There shouldn't be, but there will,' he pronounced with a quick glance in her direction.

Was he thinking that he might have been guilty of human error himself? she wondered. Because Bryce was making one big mistake if he couldn't admit that what they had between them was too precious to waste.

'About Christmas—' he was saying.

'Yes,' she interrupted. 'What about it? Have you made any plans?'

Fabia was conscious that it was crunch time. If he had made plans, and she and Jessica weren't included, she would know that nothing had changed.

'Yes and no.'

'What does that mean?'

'I could be Santa Claus for Jessica on Christmas

Eve and Christmas morning, but I can't be around the rest of the time. What about you?'

'We have nothing planned,' she told him with the feeling that something was being left unsaid.

'Would you be happy with me coming round?'

She would be happy if he only turned up for five minutes, she thought wryly, but what else was he doing?

CHAPTER NINE

DURING the first week in December Bryce called in at the centre to ask if Fabia would do him a favour, and when she heard what it was she eyed him in surprise.

'A dozen or so of us on the flight staff had arranged to go for a meal before Christmas at one of the big hotels,' he explained, 'but it's been cancelled. Catastrophically for the management they've had to close the place down over the Christmas period due to some serious structural faults, which means that we've been left high and dry as no one else can fit us in so near to the time.

'In a moment of madness I've told them we'll have a party at my place instead, as I'm the one most central to the airport and have no other domestic commitments. It's not the kind of thing I usually go in for, though, and I wondered if you would help me out.'

'Me!' she exclaimed. 'In what way?'

With a vision of herself standing over a hot stove for a considerable number of hours, the prospect, while appealing in one way, was daunting in others.

As if he'd read her mind, Bryce was smiling.

'I'm having the food brought in. I'm asking for your assistance in a more relaxed context.. Will you host the party with me? The folk from the airline will be bringing their partners so it will be mostly couples.'

They could be a 'couple' if he would only say the word, she thought, but she'd been down that road once too often. Bringing her mind back on track, she asked, 'Willow, too?'

She hadn't seen the other woman since the day of the incident on the tarmac, but their fraught concern for the same man on that occasion had created a bond of sorts.

'Yes. Willow has just got engaged to some guy who's in Admin at the airport.'

'So there *are* some people who are risk-takers?'

Bryce was still smiling, as if the barb had passed him by.

'Yes, it would appear so,' he agreed smoothly. 'So what about it, Fabia? Do you think Maggie would have Jessica for the night?'

She couldn't fault him when it came to Jess, she thought. He always had her welfare at heart. If he considered her own feelings to the same degree it would be...

He was waiting for an answer and, of course, she was going to say yes. For one thing, Bryce had never seen her really dressed up. He'd always seen her as a nurse at the airport or as Jessica's mother, but there was another Fabia that he had yet to be introduced to.

'Yes, of course I'll do it,' she told him with her voice lifting. 'Just as long as Maggie will have Jess. When is it?'

'Saturday.'

'So soon!'

'Well, yes. We only got the cancellation from the hotel yesterday. Thanks for offering to help me out, Fabia.'

'Thank you for asking me. What time do you want me there?'

'Sevenish, if that's all right with you.'

She'd been free when he'd come in, but it was never for long. At that moment a middle-aged woman came limping into the centre with blood running down her leg.

'I've got an ulcer on my leg and I've just caught it on a luggage trolley,' she said agitatedly. 'The skin around it is so thin it breaks at the slightest knock. Can you do something with it, Nurse, or it will be bleeding all the time I'm in the air?'

'Yes, come this way,' Fabia told her, taking her arm, and to Bryce in a quick aside, 'I'll phone you later in the week.'

For the rest of the day Fabia was happy. Whatever the circumstances of the invitation, she was going to be spending some time with Bryce, and it was something to look forward to.

'Of course I'll have Jessica,' Maggie said when she asked her. 'You don't go out often enough. It's time you had a social life…and with your gorgeous pilot, too,' she teased.

Fabia sighed. 'I wish he was.'

'What? Gorgeous?'

'No—mine.'

Maggie knew what had happened long ago, that Bryce had been married to Tiffany, and she sympathised with the complexities of the situation. But she also thought that Bryce was crazy if he let it get in the way of their happiness.

'Your relationship's improving, though, isn't it?' she questioned.

'Yes, I suppose so,' Fabia agreed doubtfully. 'If you count the fact that we seem to be better at being friends than lovers. I wish I knew what was going on in his mind half the time. This party, for instance. It's not like Bryce to volunteer for such a thing. In the old days he was outgoing and friendly, but he's changed and is now a very private person.'

'It's up to you to break down the barriers, then, isn't it?' her friend said with a smile.

Fabia had been right when she'd said that hosting the party wasn't what she would have expected from him. He'd made the gesture on impulse, although he did have his reasons.

One had been that he had no family and so wasn't as bogged down with Christmas preparations like the others. He also didn't want to see his colleagues disappointed. But the main reason had been because he wanted some time with Fabia, and having put himself out of reach he was now wishing that he hadn't done so.

She and Jessica were going to be the bright stars of his Christmas, but he had a feeling that he wouldn't be shining very brightly in Fabia's eyes.

He'd told her he would be able to spend Christmas Eve and the following morning with them, and would have liked to have explained what he would be doing for the rest of the time as she and Jessica were the most important people in his life. But it wasn't the right time to tell Fabia what he was committed to. He had to do this thing on his own first.

So having her with him at the party was going to make up for the time he wouldn't be spending with her over Christmas, and if she thought he had a cheek, picking her up and putting her down when it suited him, he would have only himself to blame.

On the Saturday morning of the party, Fabia took Jessica along with her to the hairdresser's. She usually wore her hair long and loose, but for the evening ahead she wanted to wear it swept up into a sophisticated chignon.

The only evening dress she possessed was black with a soft, low-cut bodice and a brocade skirt. She'd had few occasions to wear it over the years, yet when she tried it on it still looked surprisingly fashionable. And with the new hairstyle, high-heeled sandals and an evening bag to match, she felt she wouldn't be letting Bryce down.

He had to wait at home for the caterer and so couldn't pick her up, and as she drove back into the city the anticipation of the evening took hold of her.

She supposed it ought to be the other way round. She should be piqued that he wanted her in his life for some things and not others. But an opportunity like this mightn't happen again, and as Maggie had said…she didn't get out enough.

When Bryce opened the door to her he caught his breath and Fabia watched his smile of welcome dwindle.

'You look too beautiful for your own good,' he said slowly, and she knew instantly that he was making a comparison.

Dismay was washing over her and there was anger with it.

'You mean I look like my sister?'

'No, I didn't mean that,' he said in a low voice. 'You took my breath away for a moment. You have a special kind of beauty that's all your own, Fabia, no matter what you wear, but tonight you look—'

He didn't get the chance to finish. There were voices outside and car doors slamming.

'Let me take your wrap,' he said quickly, and when he opened the door to the first of the visitors they were side by side, smiling serenely as if heated words had never been spoken.

Bryce's friends from the flight crew and their partners were a friendly lot, and as the party got under way Fabia forgot those first few awkward moments when she'd arrived.

She knew she'd brought Tiffany back to Bryce's mind. Maybe it was seeing her in evening clothes. Her mirror at the cottage had told her that she looked smart and sophisticated, and that was how Tiffany had looked all the time. She'd loved her sister, but they'd had little in common.

Bryce had organised a firework display to take place at midnight, and as she stood next to him in the moonlit garden with one of his jackets over the flimsy dress, he said softly, 'I don't know why we don't do this more often. I can see the fireworks dancing in your eyes.'

Fabia smiled up at him but made no reply. They'd been the recipients of one or two curious glances during the evening, and when she'd congratulated Willow on her engagement the other woman had said, 'Is it going to be your turn next, Fabia?'

Only Bryce could answer that, she thought. He knew how she felt. Nothing was going to change that. But she wasn't going to tell him again. The next move had to come from him.

Eventually the guests had gone. They'd cleared up after them and Bryce had just made coffee.

'So how did it go, do you think?' he asked as he seated himself beside her on the sofa.

Fabia smiled. He must know how it had gone. Everyone had said how they'd enjoyed themselves and they'd meant it. The food had been eaten with relish, the fireworks enjoyed and admired, and as the clock hovered on two o'clock she found that her eyelids were drooping.

The last thing she wanted was to fall asleep the moment they were alone, but it seemed as if some imp of mischief was bringing drowsiness upon her.

Bryce was watching her fight it and he smiled. She'd been the perfect hostess, attentive, pleasant and attractive, and now she was wilting, curling up against the cushions like a contented cat.

He knew that Jessica was staying the night at Maggie's so there was no need for Fabia to rush home, and as she finally gave in to sleep, he went to find a blanket to put over her.

When he came back with it he stood looking down on her. He could have kicked himself for being such a pain when she'd first arrived, but it had been the shock of seeing a side of her that he hadn't seen before. A side that for a brief second had reminded him of Tiffany. And Fabia had guessed his thoughts.

He bent and kissed her brow. She moved in her sleep and murmured his name, and he thought about the Christmas gift he had for her. He had a few things to give her, but one stood out from the rest and he was hoping that her reaction was going to be what he wanted it to be.

*   *   *

His first thought when he awoke in the morning was of her asleep on the sofa downstairs. In a flash he was throwing on a robe and padding towards the sitting room, eager to start the day with her around, but his eyes widened when he went in. The blanket was neatly folded and on top of it a hastily scribbled note.

It said, 'I have to get home to Jess. Didn't want to wake you. Sorry I went to sleep on you, but maybe it was for the best. Thanks for a lovely party. Love, Fabia.'

He picked up the blanket and buried his face in it. He could smell her perfume, and as his blood warmed at the thought of how close it had been to the slender sweetness of her, he knew that having her under his roof for one night wasn't enough. He wanted her there always. The fact that they'd slept in separate beds didn't matter. What counted was that she had been there.

Bryce had a night flight on Sunday but called round briefly in the afternoon to make sure Fabia had got home all right and that all was well with Jessica.

She was back to the woman he knew best when he got there, in jeans and a sweatshirt and her hair tied back in a ponytail.

As if reading his thoughts, she said laughingly, 'Yes. Cinderella is well and truly home from the ball.'

'You were great,' he said, 'and it wouldn't have been anywhere near as good without you.'

Fabia's eyes were sparkling and he thought that she was just as beautiful now as she'd been the night before.

'I've got some things for Jessica in the boot of my car,' he said in a low voice, 'and there are a couple of parcels for you just in case I don't see you before Christmas Eve. You'll be getting your most important present on Christmas morning. I hope you'll like it.'

Fabia could feel her cheeks warming. She knew what she would like it to be, but just because everything was wonderful between them at the moment, it didn't mean that he'd changed his mind.

'You've got me all curious,' she told him.

Suddenly he was serious, sombre almost.

'Well, you haven't long to wait. All will soon be revealed.'

'You said that on Christmas Day you would only be able to be with us in the morning,' she reminded him, still with the feeling that there were things being left unsaid. 'But you'll be here to have lunch with us, won't you?'

'Yes,' he said, still in serious mood. 'But I'll have to leave immediately afterwards.'

'In that case, we'll have our main meal then. Unless someone else is cooking your Christmas dinner.'

'Not that I know of,' he hedged. 'I shall enjoy eating with you and Jessica.'

Why was he being so secretive? she wondered when he'd gone. There was definitely something going on in his life that he didn't want to tell her about. If it had been that he was on duty, he would have told her. But there were very few flights, if any, out of the airport on Christmas Day, so it couldn't be that.

She sighed. At least she and Jess would have Bryce for part of Christmas. It was something to be grateful for.

*   *   *

As with every approaching holiday time the airport was getting busier and correspondingly so was the walk-in centre.

It was apparent that the general public when out of their normal environments were more prone to accidents. In many cases the sudden freedom from daily cares and routines brought about a kind of recklessness that made people less careful than they would normally be, sometimes resulting in a chastening visit to the centre.

That was how it seemed to be at the moment. A young child had pulled over a display of books in one of the airport shops while its parents had been sauntering around the counters, and had received a cut face from the metal stand the books had been resting on.

There'd been lots of tears and frightened wailing while the graze had been attended to, and the parents, now all attention, had watched in subdued silence.

An eager photographer, wanting to film his family prior to boarding, had stepped back into a luggage trolley and had twisted his leg badly. Now limping with the pain, he was bemoaning his photographic enthusiasm and hoping that he hadn't done anything serious enough to spoil his holiday.

'It's the muscle at the back of your leg that you've jarred,' Fabia told him. 'I'll put a cold compress on it for the moment and in the meantime rest it. I know there isn't a lot of leg room on an aircraft but try to keep it stretched out if you can. Muscular problems usually improve with rest. But if it gives you trouble during the holiday, you'll have to see a doctor.'

'So that's it,' he'd said thankfully. 'Just a pulled muscle.'

If those two incidents had been minor, the next one

wasn't. An elderly man had stumbled, getting off an escalator, and was lying with his leg twisted beneath him.

When the call came through Fabia hurried to the scene. An ambulance would have been sent for but in situations like this the staff from the centre had the advantage of being on the spot.

He was lying with his eyes closed, moaning, 'My leg! My leg!'

'Don't try to move, sir,' she said quickly. 'Just lie still until the ambulance arrives. Is there anyone with you?'

'No,' he said faintly. 'I'm on my way to my daughter's in Canada.'

Fabia felt his pulse. It wasn't strong and a swelling was appearing on the side of his head.

'Did you bang your head as you fell?' she asked, feeling his bony skull with gentle hands.

'Yes, I think so,' he mumbled. 'I can't remember.'

At that moment Giles appeared, and as he dropped down beside her he said, 'What have we here?'

'Possible fracture of the left leg,' she told him, then pointed to the swelling at the side of his head. 'And maybe a haematoma.'

He'd brought a blanket with him, and as they placed it over the victim the man's breathing became shallower and his skin felt cold and clammy.

'He's going into shock,' Giles said urgently. 'Check his pulse while I make sure that his airway isn't blocked. We need an ambulance and we need it fast.'

The man's pulse was rapid and very weak. That, along with all the other signs, said that his condition was serious. At that moment there was the sound of a siren outside the building and within minutes the paramedics were joining them.

When the patient had been carefully eased onto a stretcher with his leg positioned so there would be no further damage, and had had extra blankets piled on him to restore body warmth, Fabia observed him anxiously. It was going to mean worry and disappointment for the daughter he'd been going to visit. Once he'd been treated, the hospital authorities were going to have the unenviable task of letting her know what had happened.

When the ambulance had left, Giles said, 'I have a meeting in a few minutes' time, Fabia, so I'll see you back at the centre.'

She nodded and was on the point of returning when she almost collided with Willow.

'Hi, there,' the other woman said, and as Fabia returned the greeting. 'So, what do you think about Bryce deserting us?'

'I'm afraid I'm not with you,' she said slowly.

'He's gone. Left the airline. The first we knew about it was yesterday when he told us it was his last flight—that was all he had to say. We thought that you would have known all about it as you and he are so close, but I can tell from your expression that you don't.'

Close! That would be the day if what Willow was saying was true! The word was ringing in Fabia's ears. If they *were* close, yes, she might have known what Bryce was up to. But what she was hearing proved for evermore that they were anything but that.

Where had he gone? she thought painfully. And why? Had he transferred to another airline maybe? But Willow was reading her mind.

'He said that it was his last day at the airport so it looks as if he's severed all connections with the job. Maybe you'll let us know what's happening when he gets in touch.'

'Er…yes…I will,' she agreed weakly as shock waves hit her.

As if to confuse her further, the flight purser said, 'I have to go, but one more thing…his house is up for sale. I saw the sign as I drove past this morning, so it looks as if he really means to leave everything behind. Maybe he's decided to move to Cornwall, do you think?'

'I'm sure I don't know,' Fabia told her.

There was a bitter taste in her mouth. So this was what it was all about, she thought bleakly as she continued on her way with dragging steps. How could he do it to her? Make such final arrangements without a word?

She'd known from the moment of meeting him again that he was a changed man and had understood, even though she'd been sad at the waste of his charm and talents. But this was keeping his life separate from her to a new dimension.

What would Jessica say when she knew he'd gone? It hadn't been long since she'd been filled with dread at having to tell her daughter that Bryce was no more when there'd been the incident of the faulty undercarriage.

This was less serious but no less devastating. Yet he must have a good reason for what he'd done, she told herself as optimism surfaced. He might call in at the centre to explain his actions or be waiting for her at home. Or at least have left a note.

But by the evening none of those things had happened, and Fabia rang his house. She'd been longing to do it all day but had stubbornly refrained, telling herself that it was his place to get in touch with her. He did at least owe her that before he went on to the new life that he appeared to be planning.

There was no answer and as the phone rang and rang the sound echoed emptily in her ear. Anger had her in its grip now. The feeling that she'd been used was almost choking her.

She had no doubts about his love for Jessica, but with regard to herself she'd never been sure what his feelings were until now. He must have known he'd be leaving his job and putting the house on the market for days, weeks even, and he'd not said a word.

When he'd brought their Christmas presents Bryce had said it was just in case he didn't see them before Christmas. She'd thought nothing of it at the time, as she'd known he was going to be there on Christmas Eve and the morning of Christmas Day, but what was going to happen now?

It was only three days away. Would he keep his promise? And if he did, what sort of an atmosphere would there be between them? Was the special gift that she was to receive the news that he was moving on? Would he expect her to be pleased for him?

He needed some lessons in sensitivity if it was. She'd thought that this Christmas was going to be one of the best ever, but it was turning out to be a disaster before it had even begun.

All the time during the countdown to Christmas Eve Fabia was on tenterhooks. Praying every time the door opened at the centre that it might be Bryce. At home rushing to answer the doorbell or the phone every time they rang, and all the time keeping a smiling face for Jessica.

But it was as if he'd disappeared off the face of the earth, and with each passing minute she became more convinced that he wouldn't be with them over Christmas.

Willow had called in at the centre to say that none of the flight staff had heard anything of him since he'd left, and had Fabia?

'No. I'm afraid not,' Fabia told her. 'It would seem that Bryce has already gone to wherever he is going.'

'Have you tried the house in Cornwall?'

'Yes,' she admitted reluctantly, having no wish to let Willow see how miserable she was.

'This isn't like him,' the other woman said. 'He's not the type for leaving loose ends.'

'Well, he hasn't, has he?' Fabia commented drily. 'He's said his farewells to you and the other flight crew, and obviously sees our relationship as easily dispensable.'

'I wouldn't have thought that to be the case,' Willow responded, 'but it does look like it and I'm so sorry. I would have said that you and he were perfect for each other.'

When she'd gone Fabia felt more despondent than ever. That the day should dawn when Willow was trying to console her over Bryce was incredible. There'd been a time when she'd thought that Willow had been making a play for him, but he'd assured her that it hadn't been so and her subsequent engagement had backed it up.

On the evening of that same day those staff who weren't on duty at the centre were meeting for a

Christmas drink in a wine bar in the city. Maggie had agreed to sit in with Jessica so Fabia had promised to go, but as she dressed for the occasion her heart wasn't in it.

They would all be in high spirits and she would be like a damp squib in their midst, she kept telling herself. Giles was a kind soul and he'd asked a few times if everything was all right, having observed that a certain pilot had been absent of late.

'Yes. I'm fine,' she'd told him.

The last thing she wanted those she worked with to discover was that she'd been well and truly dumped by the man she was in love with.

By eleven o'clock she'd had enough and, making her excuses, went to find her car. It was pointing in the direction of home, but on impulse she turned it round and within minutes was parked outside Bryce's house.

She'd half expected it to be ablaze with light, as if mocking her misery, but it was dark and still. The only bright splash of colour was the estate agent's board beside the gate, announcing that the property was for sale.

Changing jobs wasn't such a final thing to do, she thought despondently, but putting the house up for sale at the same time was. Where was he, she wondered, and why had he left without saying goodbye?

She would still have wished him well, even though he was breaking her heart. Bryce deserved to be happy. He was strong, honourable, loving when he would let himself be and had never hurt anyone…until now.

A passing police car slowed and reversed until it drew level.

'You all right, madam?' one of the two officers inside asked her.

Fabia managed a smile.

'Yes, thanks, Officer. I called to see a friend but it looks as if he's either not at home or has moved.'

'Best not to hang about, then,' he said, and, as they obviously weren't going to go until she did, Fabia had no choice but to direct herself towards home.

As Christmas drew nearer, it was brought home to her, as it always was, that she wasn't the only one with problems. Right up to the last moment on the morning of Christmas Eve travellers were coming into the centre with their health and fitness problems.

It had been a cold night and a heavy frost was still glistening on the roads and pavements outside the airport, but inside it was the usual bustle and today it was tempered with anxiety in case the weather conditions prevented flights taking off.

They'd already had a teenage girl who'd slipped on the ice and sustained a dislocated shoulder as she'd been retrieving her luggage from a taxi.

And arriving on an inward flight from Africa, a British businessman had developed a raging fever on the journey and was shivering as if with ague when he walked into the centre, even though his temperature was sky high.

'I know I should have consulted my GP,' he said through chattering teeth, 'but this late there'll be no more surgeries until after Christmas, and in any case I feel so ill I don't think I could have made it.'

'That's what we're here for,' Fabia told him with a smile. 'To deal with problems for people who need or want to be treated on the spot. Though, looking at

you, I think you will be requiring more than our re-
sources can provide.'

When questioned he confirmed that he'd had all the
necessary injections, but it still looked like the onset
of a tropical disease. If Fabia had been asked for an
opinion she would have said malaria, having seen it
a few times previously. She knew that even after taking precautions a visitor to the tropics could still catch
it.

'Don't tell me I'm going to be hospitalised over
Christmas,' the man groaned as he heard Giles phon-
ing for an ambulance.

'It looks like it,' she told him sympathetically.

When Fabia finished work in the early afternoon there
was an urgency in her to get away from the airport.
A couple of pilots homeward bound had called in at
the centre earlier. She'd recognised one of them as
being a friend of Giles's whom they'd treated for a
couple of minor ailments some weeks earlier. He was
dropping off a bottle of sherry for the staff.

They'd been cheerful and relaxed, happy to be
leaving flight duties and gold braid behind for a couple of days, and she'd thought miserably that there
were too many reminders of Bryce around the place.
Yet did she want to go home and have to cope with
Jessica wanting to know when he was coming?

Anger at what he'd done kept washing over her. It
was there now as she thought that Bryce could treat
her how he liked, but to let Jessica down was another
matter, and if ever she did see him again he would
hear about it.

Yet there was still time. She didn't really believe

he would come but he might. Maybe he would come striding into the cottage, bringing a waft of cold night air with him, and turn a drab day into a special occasion. But she would still want some answers.

CHAPTER TEN

AFTER doing her last-minute shopping, Fabia found herself arriving home to problems. Jessica had been at Maggie's all morning and now it was her turn to look after the three children while her friend made her last visit to the shops before the festivities began.

But there was nothing festive about Maggie's expression when Fabia went next door and the children, instead of playing, were standing around looking apprehensive.

'What's wrong?' she asked, and her neighbour immediately burst into tears.

'It's my mum. I've just had a phone call to say a neighbour found her and she could barely move. She's been rushed into hospital. I have to go to her, Fabia. You know that Dad died last year so she's all alone up there in Tyneside.'

Maggie's glance went to the boys who were observing her solemnly as they tried to grasp the seriousness of what was happening. 'Daddy will be home any minute and he'll look after you,' she said on a sob.

'You can't drive all that way in the state you're in,' Fabia told her. 'Let him take you and I'll have the boys.'

'But it's Christmas,' Maggie protested. 'And I know you've got yours all planned. It wouldn't be fair to—'

'Shush,' Fabia said gently. 'Go and pack a few

things so that you'll be ready when their father gets here. Don't worry about my plans. At the moment they're very much up in the air.'

As Maggie gave her a grateful hug she whispered, 'The children's presents are on the top of the wardrobe in our bedroom. I'll ring as soon as we get there. And Fabia…thanks.'

'You don't need to thank me,' Fabia told her. 'I owe you a lot.'

By half past three Maggie and her husband were on their way, and Fabia was left with the children. They'd gone up to Jessica's bedroom to play, their earlier uncertainties forgotten in the excitement of the coming night, and as Fabia looked around her she was thinking that all her preparations were done. The tree was up and decorated, swags of holly and mistletoe graced the window-sills and outside coloured lights twinkled on the trees. The larder was stocked and a turkey was waiting to be cooked.

As winter twilight descended, she told herself that only one thing was missing. The presence of the man she loved.

When the phone rang she picked it up slowly, challenging the fates to disappoint her again.

'Fabia?' Bryce's voice said in her ear with a sort of tight precision.

'Yes?' she croaked.

'I'm not going to be able to make it. Something has come up. I'm so sorry.'

She was gathering her wits. 'Don't be,' she told him coldly. 'I wasn't expecting you in any case after your disappearing act.'

'So you know I've left my job.'

'Yes, Willow told me.'

'I was hoping that you wouldn't come across any of the flight crew just yet.'

'So if I hadn't met her you would have expected me not to notice that you'd disappeared from the scene,' she said tartly. 'You've put your house up for sale, too. Am I entitled to know what is going on? I thought we were friends, but I've come to the conclusion that trusting me is something you still aren't prepared to do.'

'We *are* friends. I *do* trust you.'

'You have a funny way of showing it.'

He sighed.

'Yes. I suppose I have. It's just that everything isn't working out how I'd planned it.'

'Oh, I don't know. From where I'm standing it looks as if you've got it all sorted,' she remarked drily, with a sick feeling that she was handling it all wrong yet didn't know why. 'Willow commented that you are a person who doesn't like loose ends, but it looks to me as if they are all neatly tied, with the exception of giving me the brush-off. And now that you've done that, you can go ahead with whatever you've been planning.'

'I have to go,' he said, without attempting to defend himself and with a catch in his voice. 'Tell Jessica I love her and that I hope she likes her presents.'

'You have some nerve!' she exclaimed, but the line was dead. He'd gone and, slumping down onto the nearest chair, she wept for what could have been.

The children were asleep. They'd been excited at the thought of Santa being somewhere around in the skies and had taken ages to settle down, but at last there was silence in the house and as Fabia sat beside the fire, having a last cup of coffee before going to bed herself, she switched on the television to catch the late-night local news.

The main item was a report on a coach crash that had taken place as a group of pensioners had been returning from a visit to a pantomime in the city centre. On their way home on a lonely country road the driver had dozed off at the wheel and the coach had ended up in a ditch.

There were many casualties and the accident and emergency unit at the Infirmary had been placed on red alert, with extra staff being brought in.

What had happened to the unfortunate passengers made her own state of misery seem trivial, but as with the holidaymakers who came unstuck at the airport just when they should have been at their happiest, so it was with Christmas-time, she thought. There was always sorrow for someone.

Maggie had phoned an hour ago to say that her mother's problem had turned out to be polymyalgia rheumatica, a severe muscular illness that older women were prone to, and she might be allowed home the next day once she'd been put on a course of steroids.

'We're going to bring her back with us once she's discharged,' her friend had said, 'otherwise I'll have no peace of mind, with Mum living on her own. It's quite a serious thing that she's got. When her neighbour found her she could hardly move.'

She'd asked tearfully about the boys and had brightened up when Fabia had told her they were fine, tucked up in bed and asleep.

'We'll ring in the morning to speak to them,'

Maggie had said. 'And what about you, Fabia? Is Bryce with you?'

'No. He rang to say that he can't make it.'

Fabia hadn't gone into details. Not even Maggie was going to know how hurt and lost she was feeling, but her friend hadn't let the subject drop.

'Oh, that's a shame!' she'd exclaimed. 'I know how much you were looking forward to spending part of Christmas with him. Is everything all right between you?'

'Yes, fine,' Fabia had fibbed.

Maggie had enough on her mind without a recital of her own woes. By the time they got her mother here, if the hospital did discharge her on Christmas Day, the holiday would be nearly over. They would have missed seeing the boys open their Christmas presents and would be coming back to rearrange their lives so that a sick elderly woman could be cared for.

When Fabia went to bed there was no sleep in her. Lying wide-eyed beneath the eaves, she kept turning the events of the day over in her mind.

It had been a day that had brought disappointment and despair as far as she and Bryce were concerned, and for Maggie there had been great anxiety, resulting in her being many miles away on this Christmas Eve.

And Bryce? She didn't know where he was. She'd thought she knew him but had realised how wrong she was. But at least he'd phoned her. Broken into the dreadful void he'd created. She supposed she should be thankful for that.

Sleep came at last and it seemed to her that she'd barely closed her eyes before she heard small feet padding along the landing.

Loud whispers indicated that the children were trying not to wake her up as they crept down the stairs. Loth to face a new day without Bryce, Fabia lay there, listening to their gigglings and scufflings.

There'd been some sad Christmas Days in the past but this was in a class of its own, she thought as daylight crept through the curtains. All her bright hopes had finally gone down the drain.

But there were three young innocents downstairs, opening their packages, and she wasn't going to let her gloom descend on them so, throwing on a robe and flicking a brush through her hair, she sallied forth.

Listening to the children's cries of delight, she found her mood lightening. It was their day and as long as her beloved Jess accepted without tears that Bryce wasn't going to be with them, and Maggie's boys' excitement blotted out the fact that they, too, were missing their parents, she would cope.

She'd decided that they would have the main meal in the evening now that Bryce wasn't coming and a snack at lunchtime so that the children could play with their toys uninterrupted.

The boys from next door had both found new skateboards amongst their presents, and within minutes of opening them they were dressed and out on the garden path, whizzing along in high glee, while Jessica was dressing and undressing her dolls in new outfits before placing them in the cot that Bryce had bought her.

There'd been other gifts from him, too, which Fabia could tell had been chosen with care and no lack of expense. Yet, she thought miserably, he couldn't be bothered to be there to see the child open them.

It was late morning. The turkey was in the oven,

the vegetables prepared and she'd just placed a plate full of sandwiches on the kitchen table when there was a cry from outside where the two boys were still playing on their skateboards.

When she ran out to see what was wrong Fabia found Paul, the youngest, lying on the path with his arm twisted beneath him. He was howling with pain and she knew that the downside of this particular Christmas was still intent on making itself felt.

She could tell by the way his arm was bent that it was a fracture, and at the same moment as the depressing thought of spending the afternoon in Accident and Emergency came to mind she was helping him carefully to his feet.

When the ambulance came the paramedics were chirpy and cheerful as they placed the injured arm in a temporary sling. When Fabia explained that they would all be going with them as there was no one she could leave the other two children with, they nodded understandingly and said what a shame that their day was being spoilt.

Their own day wouldn't exactly be a laugh a minute, she thought gratefully, having to work on Christmas Day, and it would be the same for the staff manning the casualty department.

'I imagine you were busy last night with the coach-crash victims,' she said as they sped to the infirmary along almost deserted roads.

'It was bedlam,' one of them informed her. 'Still is very busy as there were the usual casualties as well to be attended to. The operating theatres were occupied non-stop all night. Some of the doctors who were on duty at the time of the crash are still treating people.'

'So you think we'll have a long wait?' she questioned anxiously.

'Not with a youngster in pain,' he said. 'They usually see them right away.'

He was right. After being seen by the triage nurse, they were taken to a cubicle and told, 'The doctor will be with you shortly.'

Fabia knew the procedure well enough. After being examined by the doctor, they would be sent to have the injured arm X-rayed. If it was a clean break, a cast would follow.

She prayed that it would be a straightforward fracture. That in itself would be bad enough news to have to tell Paul's parents.

After helping the young boy carefully onto the bed, Fabia took stock of the rest of them. Jessica and his older brother were gazing around them wide-eyed, lost for words at the unexpected turn of events. And as for herself, she'd thrown on an old raincoat from the hall cupboard and was still wearing the fluffy mules she'd put on first thing.

Her smile was wry. To the onlooker they must seem a sorry quartet. But none of that mattered. What counted was that Paul was treated with speed and efficiency.

She couldn't believe that this had happened while she'd been responsible for him. It wasn't as if the children had never had skateboards before. They were used to them and the falls that went with them. The amount of damage depended on how they fell and this time it had been serious.

She could hear footsteps approaching the cubicle. The next moment the curtains were swished back to admit a tall figure in a white coat, and as Fabia's face went slack with amazement her world began to right itself.

It was as if bells were pealing, angel choirs singing on high. Answers to her tortured questions were being given all in that split second.

Bryce's amazement equalled her own. He'd seen the name on the admission form but not knowing her neighbour by anything other than 'Maggie', it hadn't registered.

And now here they were—Fabia looking pale-faced and transfixed, Jessica beaming her delight and the injured boy fixing him with the woebegone expression of a child who was wishing he'd been more careful.

'Fabia,' he breathed. 'I've been trying to get hold of you for the last half-hour, but it's not surprising there was no answer if you were on your way here. The crisis is over and those of us who've been on duty all night are finishing in a few minutes' time when a new shift takes over.'

He flashed her an apologetic smile. 'I know I've got a lot of explaining to do but I never thought I'd be doing it here. I'd planned to tell you what I've been up to in more romantic surroundings than this. So, tell me what's happened. Why are you in charge of Maggie's children?'

She'd been speechless with joy. Bryce was back where he belonged…in health care, but now she had to get down to basics.

'She's in Newcastle. Her mother was taken to hospital yesterday so I said I'd have the boys. They both had new skateboards amongst their presents. Need I say more?'

Her voice sounded as if it was coming from far

away. She was transfixed with the magic of the moment, the exquisite pleasure of seeing him, being with him, hearing him. It was like finding her way out of the desert to a fertile land.

Bryce was examining the injured arm with gentle fingers and when he lifted his head he said, 'It's almost certainly a fracture. We're lucky that Radiology is open. Two of the staff who weren't expecting to be working on Christmas Day volunteered to come in when they heard about the coach crash, so let's go and see what they can do for us, shall we?'

As they all walked along the hospital corridor, with Jessica clinging tightly to his hand, he said in a low voice, 'This was to have been my gift to you. It still is, but you've taken the surprise out of it. I was going to offer you my contract of employment tied up with ribbon this morning, but you know what they say about the best-laid plans.

'I applied to be taken back into medicine some weeks ago and was offered this appointment in A and E. I'm having to do some retraining to run parallel with hands-on treatment, which will bring me up to date with what's been happening in the years I've been out of the service. And here I am.'

'Yes, here you are,' Fabia said softly.

He smiled.

'It was my idea to disappear for a few days so as to keep the surprise for today. I hoped that you wouldn't notice I wasn't around for that short time, but I reckoned without you bumping into Willow and the only way I could keep my secret intact after that was to stay out of sight until Christmas Eve. But the crisis last night put paid to me spending it with you and I had my doubts about today. Though, if we're going to spend our lives together, we'll need to expect that kind of thing.'

Fabia was silent, but her eyes were full.

They arrived at the X-ray unit, and as the radiologist took over Fabia sank down onto the nearest chair and looked up at him with questioning violet eyes.

'Tell me that you haven't done this just to please me,' she begged. 'I know how much you love flying.'

'I've done it because everything you've ever said to me suddenly made sense and I realised what was really important to me. Yes, I do love flying, but from now on it will be my hobby rather than my job. Much as I enjoyed working for the airline, there was always the thought that there was something else that I'd also trained for, which, when I thought back to it, had been the most rewarding thing I'd ever done in my life. My values have changed since I met you again, Fabia. You've brought light and peace to the dark recesses of my mind.'

'So it doesn't matter who I am? What my origins are?' she questioned.

'No. It's as you once said to me…you are your own person, not a clone of someone else.'

'And you can see me as a doctor's wife?'

The radiologist was bringing the young casualty back to them and Jessica and Paul's brother were both agog as to what was to happen next, so Bryce's reply had to be brief. But it didn't stop them from being words of wonder and there was a promise in his eyes that she couldn't mistake as he said softly, 'Yes. As long as the doctor in question is me.'

Bryce studied the x-rays and to Fabia's relief reported that it was a straightforward fracture of the humerus.

'There won't be any need for pinning or any other kind of operation,' he said. 'They'll put a temporary cast on and then we can all go home.'

'I've got the unenviable task of telling his mum and dad what's happened when we get back,' she said soberly as they left the hospital. 'As if Maggie hasn't got enough to worry about already.'

'She'll be aware that skateboarding can be dangerous,' he pointed out. 'This young fellow is the third I've treated for skateboard injuries this week.'

Fabia nodded. It was true, but she would be relieved to get it off her chest. The opportunity to do that came sooner than expected.

A car was in Maggie's drive when they got home. Her neighbours were back. A frail elderly lady was sitting by the fire with a cup of tea when they all went trooping in. Explanations were given and Paul suitably fussed over, and now it was time for the two families to separate.

Fabia invited the others to join them for their Christmas meal but Maggie said, 'No. There is a glow about you that tells its own story. The two of you need some time alone. Leave Jessica here with us for a while. Later, if there are any turkey or mince pies going begging, we wouldn't say no.'

The moment the door of the cottage had closed behind them Bryce placed a small gift-wrapped box in Fabia's hand.

'A belated merry Christmas, Fabia,' he said as her eyes widened. 'This is the other part of my gift to you. I hope you'll accept it, and my proposal of marriage. I love you, Fabia. Will you be my wife?'

'Of course I will, Bryce. You already know how much I love you.'

Fabia opened the package and gasped when she saw the sparkling diamond ring inside.

'Let me put it on,' he said tenderly. 'Until I see it on your hand, I won't really believe you're mine.'

'I've been yours for a very long time, Bryce,' she said softly as she held out her hand for him to place the solitaire on her finger. 'But only I knew that. The ring is beautiful. Now I can tell the world.'

'You were the most beautiful sight I'd ever seen when I walked into that cubicle at the hospital,' he murmured as he held her close.

She laughed up at him.

'In my old mac and with my mules all squelchy from the hospital car park?'

'Yes.'

'I still can't believe it,' she said dreamily.

'What can't you believe?'

'That you love me.'

'I'm afraid you have to. We're going to be together always, Fabia. Isn't that a wonderful thought?'

'Yes, it is, but there's something I don't understand.'

'And what is that?'

'Why have you put your house up for sale?'

'I thought that the sooner it was sold, the sooner we could buy a place of our own. Unless you want to stay here. I've been using hospital accommodation in the meantime.'

'I don't care where I live as long as it's with you,' she told him tenderly. 'I've waited a long time for this. I can't remember a time when I didn't love you.'

'You've no idea how many times I've told myself I don't deserve you,' he said, holding her even closer.

'I thought that you were still dubious about my family ties.'

'The only person I had doubts about was myself. Whether I could make you happy. You've shown me how to trust again. How to forgive. I spent all those years feeling sorry for myself when all the time you were having to face bringing up a fatherless child on your own. If you'll marry me, Jessica will be the icing on the cake.'

'I've already told you I'll marry you,' she said softly, 'and I'll give you babies of your own, God willing, but before I make any more promises there's something I have to do.'

'And what's that?'

'Take the turkey out of the oven,' she told him laughingly. 'If you don't want a burnt offering.'

'And then we'll go and get Jessica and tell Maggie and her family our good news,' he suggested.

Fabia nodded. 'I can't wait to see Jess's face.'

'So you don't think she'll mind?'

'Mind! She'll be ecstatic.'

'And you?'

'Need you ask?' she said with sparkling eyes, and after that there was no need for words. Bryce's kisses said it all.

His house had been sold and Bryce was still living in hospital accommodation until the wedding. Fabia had wanted him to move into the cottage with them until they found a bigger place of their own, but he'd said, 'No. I can wait until we're married. I want us to start our lives together on an equal footing, not with me as your lodger.' With a look that made her melt with longing he added, 'But the sooner we find somewhere, the better.'

And now they had—a converted barn at the other end of the village. Always with Jessica's welfare in mind, he'd suggested that they find somewhere local so that she didn't have to change schools and would still be near Maggie's boys, and Fabia had agreed wholeheartedly.

Jessica was to be her bridesmaid and in the absence of any close male relatives Maggie would be giving her away. Bryce's friend and co-pilot Jack, who had made a slow but sure recovery from the heart attack he'd suffered the day of the crash-landing, was to be best man.

And on a cold, crisp day in February it all came together in the village church. The marriage of the doctor and the nurse, whose love for each other was plain to see as the bride in a long dress of cream brocade came down the aisle on the arm of her friend, followed by a beaming bridesmaid.

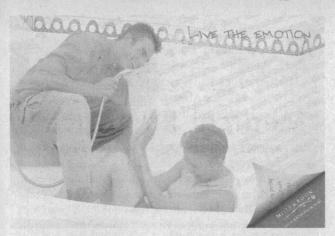

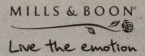

MILLS & BOON®
Live the emotion

Medical Romance™

OUTBACK ENGAGEMENT *by Meredith Webber*

Outback vet Tom Fleming has a problem. After featuring in a magazine as the 'Lonely Country Bachelor' he is surrounded by would-be wives! Merriwee's new doctor, Anna Talbot, is beautiful, blonde and engaged. Perhaps Tom should claim that *he* gave her the ring – having a fake fiancée may end all his woman troubles…

THE PLAYBOY CONSULTANT *by Maggie Kingsley*

Surgeon David Hart puts commitment into work rather than relationships. So he's surprised by his turn-about in feelings when his senior registrar turns out to be Dr Rachel Dunwoody, the woman who walked out on him six years ago! David has some urgent questions. Why did she leave? And, most urgently, how can he get her back?

THE BABY EMERGENCY *by Carol Marinelli*

When Shelly Weaver returned to the children's ward as a single mum, she discovered it was Dr Ross Bodey's first night back too. On discovering her newly single status he'd come back – for her! Suddenly Ross was asking her to change her life for ever – yet Shelly had her son to consider now. Could she make room for them both in her life?

On sale 7th November 2003

Available at most branches of WHSmith, Tesco, Martins, Borders, Eason, Sainsbury's and all good paperback bookshops.

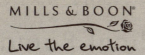

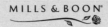

4 FREE

books and a surprise gift!

We would like to take this opportunity to thank you for reading this Mills & Boon® book by offering you the chance to take FOUR more specially selected titles from the Medical Romance™ series absolutely FREE! We're also making this offer to introduce you to the benefits of the Reader Service™—

- ★ FREE home delivery
- ★ FREE gifts and competitions
- ★ FREE monthly Newsletter
- ★ Exclusive Reader Service discount
- ★ Books available before they're in the shops

Accepting these FREE books and gift places you under no obligation to buy, you may cancel at any time, even after receiving your free shipment. Simply complete your details below and return the entire page to the address below. *You don't even need a stamp!*

YES! Please send me 4 free Medical Romance books and a surprise gift. I understand that unless you hear from me, I will receive 6 superb new titles every month for just £2.60 each, postage and packing free. I am under no obligation to purchase any books and may cancel my subscription at any time. The free books and gift will be mine to keep in any case.

M3ZEE

Ms/Mrs/Miss/Mr ....Initials.....................................
BLOCK CAPITALS PLEASE

Surname ....

Address ....

....

....Postcode..............................

Send this whole page to:
UK: FREEPOST CN81, Croydon, CR9 3WZ
EIRE: PO Box 4546, Kilcock, County Kildare (stamp required)